A Place
for Jeremy

A Place for Jeremy

by Patricia Hermes

HARCOURT BRACE JOVANOVICH, PUBLISHERS

San Diego   New York   London

J F

Library of Congress Cataloging-in-Publication Data
Hermes, Patricia.
    A place for Jeremy.
    Sequel to: What if they knew?
    Summary: After she switches schools in the middle of the year
and goes to stay with her grandparents, eleven-year-old Jeremy's life
is further disrupted when her parents announce from overseas that
they are adopting a new baby sister for her.
    [1. Schools—Fiction. 2. Grandparents—Fiction.
3. Babies—Fiction. 4. Sisters—Fiction] I. Title.
PZ7.H4317Pl 1987   [Fic]   86-31794
ISBN 0-15-262350-7

Designed by Francesca Smith
Printed in the United States of America
First edition
A B C D E

For my son Mark, with love

A Place
for Jeremy

I was back! I was really, really back. Back to spend at least a month, maybe more, at Grandma and Grandpa's and to see my old friends. And even though it meant going to school here in Brooklyn, I didn't mind. I love it here. It's not far from where I live— on Long Island—so I come here to visit whenever I can. I'd even gone to school here last fall, and I had lots of friends. Like the twins, Mimi and Libby, and even weird little Carrie. Carrie. I hadn't thought of her in months. I wondered if she'd grown since I'd seen her, or if she was still a little shrimp. Once, last fall, she had come to school wearing a little pink dress with a big bow in the back, and littler bows all over it. Everybody said it made her look just like a baby shrimp.

Baby. I was sick of that word. That's all my parents talked about anymore. And they couldn't even just plain *have* a baby like regular parents did. No, they had to go find a baby to *adopt*. But I wasn't going to think about it today. Today was going to be fun.

I began yanking things out of my suitcase and throwing them into dresser drawers so fast that when I pulled out one drawer, it fell right out onto the floor. *Blam!*

I turned around and waited: Grandma was going to stick her head through the door to find what the noise was, and then she was going to say, "Honey, try to be more quiet."

One second, two seconds, three—

"Honey?" Grandma called, but—surprise!—she didn't come to the door.

"Sorry," I called back. "It just fell." And then I said under my breath, "Try to be more quiet."

"Try to be more quiet," Grandma said.

I laughed right out loud. Grandma's always telling me that. It's not that she's mean or grumpy or anything. I think it's just that she's old. Old people like quiet. Mom kept reminding me, before she and Daddy left for South America, that I should be especially good because Grandma wasn't as young as she used to be. That was pretty dumb, because nobody's as young as they used to be—not even me. Or Mom. I ought to tell her that—she was too old for a baby.

I went back to my unpacking, trying not to slam things even though I was hurrying. I couldn't wait to get to school to see my friends. I put my barrettes and hair stuff on the dresser, and then started to put Shakesbear, my stuffed bear, on my bed. I changed my mind and tucked him under my arm. I wanted to show him to Grandpa.

I slid the suitcase under the bed, giving it an extra kick so it wouldn't stick out. "Won't need you for a while," I said. I took Shakesbear and went out in the kitchen.

Grandma was at the stove, making hot chocolate. Grandpa was sitting at the table, smoking his pipe, waiting for me. He had come upstairs from his paint store as soon as I got there.

"Who were you talking to in there?" Grandma said as I sat down next to Grandpa. "Yourself?"

"No. To my suitcase," I said, laughing. "Just said I wouldn't be needing it for a while."

"It might not be as long as you think," Grandma said, turning from the stove and smiling at me.

I just shrugged. I didn't care how long my parents were gone if they were going to come back with an S.B. That's what I called it to myself—S.B., for Stupid Baby.

Grandma came over to the table and poured hot chocolate into a mug. "Are you excited about what your parents are doing? Going to Colombia for the baby?"

Stupid baby, you mean. I didn't say it out loud. "I guess," I said.

I turned to Grandpa and held out my bear. "Like him?" I said. Last fall, Carrie said it was "juvenile" for somebody in fifth grade to have stuffed bears. But I don't care what she says. Sometimes, when I'm feeling lonely, like when it's nighttime and I want Mom to kiss me good night but she's away, then my stuffed animals seem just like people.

Grandpa put down his pipe and took Shakesbear from me. He held him up, looking at him very carefully, looking right into Shakesbear's eyes. Then he held him close.

After a moment, Grandpa nodded, and handed Shakesbear back to me. He did it carefully, as though Shakesbear were a real person. "Seems like a good kind of bear," he said.

"He is," I said. "Mom gave him to me."

I smiled at Grandpa. Grandpa's my best friend. I'd never tell anybody that, except maybe Mimi or Libby, because people would think it was weird to have a grown-up for a best friend. But he is. I'm named after him—Jeremy—even though I'm a girl. People even say I look like him, but I think that's pretty silly. I'm kind of skinny, and I have blue eyes and blond hair. Grandpa has brown eyes and his hair is all gray and he's sort of roundish.

Grandma sat down across the table from Grandpa and me. "I saw your friends, Mimi and Libby, the other day," she said. "I told them you were coming."

"You didn't tell them when, did you?"

"No, I just said soon."

"Good," I said, relieved. I had written to the twins and told them I was coming in February, but I didn't tell them what day because I wanted to surprise them.

4

I took a sip of my hot chocolate. It wasn't burning hot, so I gulped the rest of it fast. It was ten to three and I had to hurry. "Listen, Grandma, can I go now?" I said. "I want to be there when they get out of school."

Grandma nodded but she got that worried look that she gets sometimes. "Now, don't you be getting into anything," she said. "That Mimi. I don't know what she's up to this time, but I could tell she was up to something. I thought she'd burst when I told her you were coming soon. She kept saying, when, when, when, when, and Libby kept poking her."

Grandma turned to Grandpa then. "You know," she said. "I think Libby has a lot more sense than the other one."

Grandpa made a sound sort of like "humm" or "umm," one of those nothing sounds. I could tell Grandma thought it meant something because she nodded like they had both agreed.

Grandpa was smoking his pipe, and a puff of smoke came up from it, half covering his face. But even though he nodded back at Grandma, I could tell he was smiling. And when he saw me looking at him, he winked at me from behind his smoke screen.

I smiled back at him.

"Don't worry," I said to Grandma. "We won't get into anything. I promise."

I got up and grabbed my coat from the big walk-in closet in the kitchen. I gave Grandpa a quick kiss on the cheek and I gave Grandma a big hug to reassure her. Then I practically flew down the steps and out to the street.

Once outside I raced toward school—past Grandpa's store, past all the tall, skinny brick buildings with their weird fancy stoops and curvy railings. Past iron fences separating tiny front yards from crowded sidewalks, past the green metal bench where Mimi and Libby and I used to sit last year. Past all the old-fashioned and familiar things. I was here, I was actually here again! And now I was just dying to get to school and see the twins. Because I knew Mimi, and whatever she had planned, it would be good. Really, really good.

2

I ran all the way to school. Mimi and Libby were going to be so surprised.

Mimi and Libby are identical twins—I mean identical. They both have super-shiny brown hair and green eyes, and they're just the same size and they weigh the same. They even lost their baby teeth at exactly the same time. They look so much alike that even the teachers can't tell them apart. Sometimes that's good, because they can trick people. Other times, Mimi gets tired of people thinking she's Libby. So once, Mimi cut her hair really short. Then Libby liked the way Mimi's hair looked, so she did the same thing to hers.

Knowing Mimi, I'm sure some day she'll think of

something crazier to do. But not Libby. Mimi gets all the good ideas, and she's real brave. Libby's scared of practically everything, but still, she goes along with Mimi's ideas most of the time.

I had gotten to know the twins really well last fall when my parents were in Europe on business. That's why I was here going to school again, because my parents were away again. Only on a stupid kind of business this time.

They were going to Colombia in South America because they'd been told by an adoption agency that they could get a baby there. They couldn't have another one of their own, and adoption agencies here in New York had told them they'd have to wait maybe years. I didn't know why they were in such a hurry. I mean, why did they need a baby anyway? I wondered if I could tell the twins about it. So far, I hadn't talked to anyone about it, not even Grandpa.

When I got to school, I stood by the fence where I'd be sure to see the twins the minute they came through the front door. Looking up at the school, I thought about how huge it was. There's hardly any kids in it anymore, because so many families have moved away, but the building's enormous. I remembered how much it had scared me the first time I had to walk in there. I wouldn't be scared tomorrow, though, when I started school again, because this time I had friends. I knew I'd be in the same class as Mimi and Libby because there are so few kids there's only one fifth grade.

Three o'clock! I heard the bell, and then the big

double doors burst open, and kids started pouring out. Little kids first. Must have been kindergarten. Geez. Kids got littler and littler every year. And then bigger kids. And then my class—Andrew! Weird Andrew! But he wasn't wearing a baseball cap the way he used to. And Michael who Mimi used to be in love with. I wondered if she still was.

And then I saw them—the twins, Mimi and Libby, and it was just like I had never left at all. They were walking out of school together, Mimi talking nonstop, Libby her head bent a little to one side, and that sort of doubtful look on her face that she gets sometimes, when Mimi is trying to talk her into something that she doesn't want to do. As usual, they weren't dressed like twins, and even I had to look real closely to see who was who—the way you tell is Mimi's chin is pointier than Libby's. But even without seeing them up close, I could tell: the one talking is practically always Mimi.

And right behind them, tagging along, shrimpy little Carrie. Then Carrie sat down on the steps to arrange her books neatly. She sure hadn't changed any. Hadn't grown any, either. I wondered if she was still a big telltale. Last year, we played a bunch of tricks on her—and that's not as mean as it sounds, because we were only getting even with her for telling on us so much. Afterward, I felt sort of sorry for her, so I tried to make friends with her. I'm not sure whether it worked or not.

I stepped into the middle of the sidewalk, right in front of Mimi and Libby.

"Hey, look out!" Mimi said, frowning. Then her face changed, and she said, "Jer—Jer—" She turned to Libby, laughing. "It's Jeremy!"

And then they both hugged me at once, and I was hugging them back, and we were all laughing and talking at the same time.

Mimi grabbed my hand and started pulling me down the walk with her. "Jeremy! I can't believe you're here! Already. And we need you. Wait'll you hear!"

"Mimi!" Libby said. "Don't start!"

"Why not? She'll love it." Mimi turned to me. "Wanna hear?"

"Hear what?"

"The stupidest idea she ever had," Libby answered for her.

"It's not stupid and you know it. It's genius," Mimi said. "You're just mad 'cause you didn't think of it first."

We had gotten around the corner from the school, and we sat down on the green metal bench that we always used to sit on.

Mimi pulled out a notebook from her backpack. The notebook was all beat-up and dirty and the wire back was coming undone, sticking out in a little spike.

"Same notebook?" I asked. The twins had made up a notebook last year that told about everyone in the class.

"Same one," Mimi said. "Look at this." She handed it to me, opened to a page. At the top it said, "Munchmore," and underneath was a whole page of stuff: blob, blubber, blimp, blich. . . . Most of it began with "bl" except the part that said how he smelled, and that began with "f."

I looked up. "Munchmore! Who's that?"

"The new music teacher," Mimi said. "Wait'll you see him. Fat City. And is he mean!"

"Is that really his name?" I asked.

"No, it's Mountmore," Libby said. "And he's not just mean; he's *super*-mean. Next to him, Dracula's friendly."

"You know what he did the other day?" Mimi said. "He makes us all put our recorders in our mouths at the same time. He says 'Go!' and we put them in, he says 'Play!' and we play. And we can't take them out till he says 'Stop.' And Julia felt sick to her stomach, and she tried to let him know, and he wouldn't listen, so she threw up right through her recorder. It sprayed out through the end and through the holes in the sides, and all over the place."

"Yuck!" I said, but I couldn't help laughing, too. "Serves him right," I said.

"Yeah, only it shoulda' hit him and it didn't," Libby said. "It mostly got Jay. You should've seen Jay trying to wipe it off the back of his head."

Mimi jumped off the bench and stood in front of us, bent over a little bit, her arms held away from her sides, swinging them slowly back and forth like she was a huge ape. "This is him," she said. "And wait'll you see him in the cafeteria. The whole time that he's going through the line he's stuffing himself.

He just takes food and eats it right off the trays. Like an electric pig."

"Yeah," Libby said, "but even so, Mimi, you can't get away with playing tricks on a teacher."

"Uh-oh," I said. It sounded like Mimi, thinking up tricks to play on a teacher. "What kind of tricks?"

"Just . . . a little joke," Mimi said. "Nothing really bad." She looked at Libby. "Anyway, Libby," she said. "I told you that you don't have to do it if you don't want. Now that Jeremy's here, she can help me."

"Help with *what?*" I asked. Knowing Mimi, I wasn't so sure I wanted to do whatever it was she had planned.

"She's having a contest," Libby said in her best grumpy voice. "For who can think up the best trick to play on Munchmore. And she's going to get in trouble, and every time she gets in trouble, so do I. Just because we're twins."

Mimi made a face at Libby and grabbed my hand. "Come on." She tugged me up to my feet. Then she poked her sister. "Come on, Lib," she said. "How about we show Jeremy around the construction site?"

From her tone of voice and the way she called Libby "Lib," I knew she was trying to make things right with Libby again. She always calls Libby "Lib" when she's trying to make up. Even though they fight a lot, they're awfully good friends.

"Yeah! Let's go." Libby jumped up. She didn't look quite so grumpy anymore.

"It's right near your grandma's," Mimi said to me. "Where they're tearing down those houses for the highway. Did your grandma tell you?"

"Course not," I said. "You know Grandma. She wouldn't want me playing there, so she wouldn't tell me about it." I laughed. "But she did say not to get into anything."

"Remember last summer when my mom said the same thing?" Mimi said.

I frowned. I didn't know what she was talking about.

"Remember?" Libby said, laughing. "She said not to get into anything, and we didn't. But Carrie did."

And then all three of us laughed. I did remember. We had tricked Carrie into getting in a dumbwaiter at the twins' house, and we sent her upstairs, but then we made her stay stuck inside the wall for a while. It was mean, but Carrie had done lots of mean things to us. We were only getting even.

"Did your grandma say anything about them tearing down her house?" Libby said.

"Grandma's house?"

"The whole block," Mimi said. "For a highway. Everybody's fighting it. The whole neighborhood's having meetings and everything."

I stopped still, right in the middle of the sidewalk. "You're kidding."

"No." They both said it at once.

"But they can't! What would happen to Grandpa's store? To their house?"

"Gone," Mimi said. "But you can stay at Libby's and my house when you come."

"No way!" I said.

"Why not?"

"I don't mean it the way it sounds. Sure I'd stay

with you. But I don't want that! I want *Grandma's* house! I want *them* to be here!"

"Well, anyway," Mimi said. "It's not happening yet."

"And you know how grown-ups are," Libby said. "They're always saying something's going to happen, but it never does."

"Sure," I said. "I guess." But I wasn't at all sure.

"Come on." Mimi put the notebook in her backpack and put the backpack over one shoulder. "Let's go to the construction place. If nobody's there, we can climb on the tractors. Race you to the corner."

We took off running, but since I'm about the fastest runner there is, I was at the corner long before either of them.

The twins came racing along, side by side, each of them shouting, "I beat you! I beat you!" And I laughed right out loud. It was just like it used to be, just like last fall. Only now somebody was talking about tearing down Grandpa's house.

3

At supper that night, Grandma talked nonstop. As usual. Grandpa was quiet. As usual. I hardly said anything at all. I just couldn't bring myself to talk about what Mimi and Libby had told me about the house. All I wanted to think about and to talk about were the good things about being back here, and I didn't want to have to worry about anything bad.

After we finished eating, Grandpa sat back and lit up his pipe. Grandma got up to get coffee and dessert. When she was across the room at the stove, Grandpa leaned close to me and said softly, "What?"

And even though I hadn't intended to, I blurted it right out loud. "Is it true they're going to tear down this house?" I asked.

Grandpa looked surprised, but before he could answer, Grandma turned from the stove and said, "Who's been filling your ears with nonsense?"

"Is it nonsense?" I asked, looking straight at Grandpa.

Grandpa shook his head. "Not nonsense," he said. "But it's not a fact yet, either. We're doing our best to keep it from happening."

"What? What are you doing?" My voice came out too loud.

"Now, Jeremy, don't go getting all upset," Grandma said, coming to the table with dessert. "It's not good for you." She cut a big piece of brownie and put it on my plate.

I didn't touch the brownie. I kept looking at Grandpa, waiting for him to tell me something more, but he was busy poking a little metal thing down inside his pipe.

Grandma sat down at the table across from me. "No sense getting excited about something you can't do anything about," she said to me, using that "let's-be-sensible" voice like Mom does sometimes. "So why don't we just have dessert?"

She picked up her fork and began to eat, but I didn't move. Sensible! How could you be *sensible* if someone was taking your house away?

After a minute, Grandma sighed and put down her fork. "I guess I have to confess—I'm just a little worried today, too," she said. "You know what was happening right out in back of the house today?"

Grandpa looked up. "What?" he said.

"Surveyors. Measuring. And from where they were putting those lines, it looked as though they were planning to go right straight through the middle of our house. Maybe right through the middle of this table." Grandma laughed, but it didn't sound happy.

Grandpa was watching her, listening and nodding. He's patient with Grandma, just like he is with me.

"Go on," he said after a minute.

"Go on? What else is there?" She made that funny, sad kind of laugh again. "This is our *home!*" She sighed. Then, suddenly, she sat up super-straight and said, "Well, there's always another place, right?" But she still had that pasted-on kind of smile, and it seemed as though she were close to tears.

I'd never seen Grandma look like that before. I turned to Grandpa.

He noticed, too. He put down his pipe, got up and came around the table. He put a hand on Grandma's shoulder. "You know home is a lot more than a *place,*" he said softly.

"I know, I know," Grandma answered. She reached up and put her hand over his.

Grandpa patted Grandma, then turned to me. He gave me a funny look—raised his eyebrows, then looked from me to Grandma—as though he were asking me to help him cheer her up.

But how could I do that? I was so worried myself. "You mean somebody can just come and decide they're going to tear your house down?" I said. "Isn't there a way you can stop it?"

Grandpa came and sat down again. "Maybe. We

have a committee that's looking into it. Right now it's not too promising, but we're not finished yet."

"But this is awful!" I said. "Where will I come visit?" I had to have a home with them, especially now. If they didn't live here in Brooklyn, where would I live when I needed to be with them? How could I see Mimi and Libby and everybody? Grandma and Grandpa *had* to live here! This was *my* home, too.

"We've been thinking about Florida," Grandma said.

"*Florida?*" I practically screamed. "But what about *me?*"

"You can visit us in Florida, too," Grandma said, using her sensible voice again.

Grandpa was shaking his head. I knew what that meant—*Grandma* had been thinking of Florida, not Grandpa.

"Well, now," Grandpa said. "There's lots of places we might consider."

"Not Florida? Near here?" I said.

"Not Florida," Grandpa said. "But not all that far, either. Maybe we'll leave Brooklyn completely. Go out to Long Island." He smiled. "We'd be closer to you then."

He lit his pipe again, then put it back in his mouth and puffed slowly for a while, as if he had to take a rest from talking. He hardly ever says that much at one time.

"What about the store?" I asked after a minute.

"Maybe it's time to retire," he said. But for the first time he looked kind of sad, and I didn't believe him.

"Retire, shmire!" Grandma shook her head. "That's why I know Florida's only a dream. You love to work and you need to work and you know it. You retire, you'll be dead in a month."

"Grandma!" I couldn't believe she'd said that.

"You mark my words." Grandma nodded at me. "That man needs to work like I need to breathe."

Grandpa sighed and I felt sorry for him. He looked so sad! Would he die without his store? I wanted to ask him, but I knew I couldn't.

"Jeremy," Grandpa said. "How're things with those friends of yours? Did you get to see anyone today?"

I knew he was trying to change the subject, but that was all right with me.

"Yes," I said. "I saw Mimi and Libby for a while."

"How are they?"

"Good."

"Were they really into any mischief?" He winked at me and sent a look toward Grandma.

I smiled for the first time since we had sat down to dinner. Grandma had been right that Mimi was up to something, and I wished I could tell him about it. But I couldn't, especially not with Grandma there. So instead, I told him about how good it was to be back, and how I was even looking forward to seeing my old teacher, Miss Gladstone, again. And then I told him what the twins had told me about what Munchmore looked like, although of course I didn't call him Munchmore. And I didn't say anything at all about Mimi's contest.

Grandpa smiled. He took his pipe out of his mouth and said quietly, "I once had a really fat teacher when I was in school. We were always thinking up tricks to play on him."

"Yeah?" I said, and I tried to sound super-casual. "Like what?"

"Oh . . . well . . . he always kept jelly beans in a jar on his desk. So one day when he wasn't there, we took marbles and mixed them in with the jelly beans and then put the whole thing back on his desk."

I laughed right out loud. "Did he put a marble in his mouth? Did he swallow it?"

Grandpa laughed. "No. But another day we all sat crooked in our chairs, leaning like we were about to fall right over onto the floor. There were maps on the wall, and we put them at an angle, too. We wanted him to think he was going crazy."

"Did it work?" I said. "Or did you get in trouble?" This wasn't a great trick, but maybe it was worth a try.

"Now stop putting ideas in her head," Grandma said, before Grandpa could answer me. "Before you know it, she'll get together with that Mimi and think up some mischief."

"Oh," he said softly. "I don't think Jeremy needs anyone to put ideas in her head." He added, so quietly that I was sure Grandma couldn't hear him, "Didn't work." He winked at me.

I smiled at him, and then I looked at Grandma. She just looked so sad sitting there. I could tell it wasn't about playing tricks on a teacher. It was still because of the house.

I turned to Grandpa again. He was watching me

watching Grandma, and I knew he knew just what I was thinking. So I said, "You know what, Grandpa? I think things with the house will work out all right."

Then I got up and started clearing the table for Grandma. Because Grandpa was right when he looked at me like that before. Grandma did need cheering up. And I didn't know any other way to do it.

After I helped with the dishes, I kissed Grandma and Grandpa good night and went to bed. I snuggled with Shakesbear, pulling him close and hugging him to me. I even kissed his little nose and mouth. He was so much like a real person. But still, I felt so lonely. I missed Mom already.

I pulled Shakesbear closer, but suddenly he didn't feel real at all anymore. So I dumped him on the floor. Right away, that made me feel guilty, so I snatched him back up and hugged him close to me again. And then I thought—at this very minute, Mom and Daddy might be holding some little kid in their arms, deciding whether or not it would be their new baby. I hated them. I hated the stupid baby. I hated the people who wanted to tear down Grandpa's house, to make them move away. I hated everybody who wanted to change things. Why couldn't people just leave things the way they were?

I took Shakesbear and flung him across the room.

4

Next day, I didn't walk to school with Mimi and Libby because I had to go early with Grandma to get re-registered. While we walked, I kept sneaking looks at her, trying to see if she still looked worried, but she acted as though she'd completely forgotten what we were talking about last night. She seemed really happy to have me here and was talking about all the things I might be doing in school for the next few months. She didn't once mention the house.

When we got to school, we went right to the office of Miss Tuller, the principal. Miss Tuller is so small, she's about my size. Which isn't all that small, but I'm only eleven. I wonder what it feels like to be old and have gray hair and still be the size of an eleven-year-old. What's special about Miss Tuller is that she's really nice—for a principal. What's weird is that practically everybody's a little scared of her. I know I am. I think it's because with some grown-ups, you know you can get away with things, and with others, you know you can't. She's one of the can'ts.

She shook my hand the way she did that first time. Then she put her other hand on top, so she was holding mine in both of hers. Her hands were soft and warm. "It's nice to have you back," she said, and I could tell she meant it.

"It's nice to be back," I said, and I meant it, too.

Then she gave me one of those looks like grown-ups do and asked, "Have you been feeling well?"

"Yes," I said. "I've been feeling *well*." It came out kind of nasty-sounding, so I added, "Thank you." I didn't mean to be rude to her.

But I knew what she was talking about. It was about that day when I got sick with the epilepsy in school last year. Epilepsy makes you faint and get shaky and make weird noises and you don't even know it's happening. Before I got my new medicine, it used to happen all the time. Kids in my other school used to make fun of me. But it happened here in school that once, and nobody laughed or anything. Except stupid little Carrie. And that's when Miss Tuller told Carrie off. Usually Miss Tuller is real formal and polite, but that day she just looked at Carrie and said, "Shut up." And Carrie did.

It was scary that day, really scary, but it hadn't

happened since. It happened because I had been forgetting to take my medicine. I hadn't been sick with the epilepsy since then, and I hadn't forgotten to take my medicine since then, either.

"She's been just fine," Grandma said. "Her mom and daddy tell me she's been doing just fine."

Miss Tuller gave me another of those long looks, but she just handed me a piece of paper to give to Miss Gladstone, the teacher, that said I was allowed back in class. Then I went outside to wait for Mimi and Libby.

It was really cold out, and before Grandma left me she kept tugging at the collar of my coat and pulling it up around my ears. I finally said, "Grandma! I'm warm enough."

She laughed. "I know," she said. "But you know what? When your daddy was a baby, whenever *I* got cold, I put a sweater on him."

"Then you better go home and put a sweater on," I said, and we both laughed.

I kissed Grandma then, and she started for home, and I went to the green bench to wait for Mimi and Libby.

There was just a little bit of snow on the ground. I found a stick and drew pictures in the snow. I wrote my name in cursive and in printing—Jeremy Martin. Lots of kids make fun of me for having a name that's a boy's name, but I don't care. I love being named after Grandpa.

"Jeremy!" someone shouted, and I looked up and there were Julia and Iris, two kids I recognized from last fall. Before I could speak, somebody had clapped two mittens over my eyes from behind.

"Guess who!"

"I don't know," I said.

"Guess!"

"Okay, okay. Uh . . . Carrie!" I knew it wasn't Carrie, because Carrie is too prissy to ever do anything like that. But I also knew it would be a good way to tease whoever it was. Practically everybody hates Carrie.

"Yuck!" The hands came away from my eyes.

I swung around. It was Jennifer and Joy. Mimi and Libby and I call them the "other" twins. They're not even sisters, but you always see them together. Joy's the rich kid, and she has a chauffeur who drives her to school on rainy days. Jennifer is the one we call Miss Perfect, because everything about her is perfect, even the way she looks. The only problem is, she knows it. We have secret names for all of them, but we like them all. I had even begun to like weird little Carrie—at least a little bit—before I left last fall. I saw her now, walking by the corner. She was the only one who didn't come over and speak to me.

"Jeremy!" Joy said. "How long are you going to be here?"

"Not sure," I said. "But at least for a while."

"Okay!" Jennifer said.

"And do we have plans," Mimi said. She had come up with Libby, and she stood there with a piece of paper in her hand. "Listen to this," she said. She read from the paper. " 'Contest! Think up the best trick to play on you-know-who.' " She looked up for a second. "Munchmore," she added.

"Yich!" Joy made a sound like she was throwing up.

"Contest entries gotta be handed to me during Math only," Mimi continued. "Enter as many times as you want. Boys can do it, too. I decide the winner. Contest deadline, Valentine's Day."

"Who's the trick on?" Carrie! That little squeaky voice couldn't be anyone else's. She's such a midget, I hadn't seen her hidden behind the others.

"Who's the trick on?" she said again, when nobody answered her.

"Not you," Libby said. "This time."

"I *know* it's not me."

"How do you know?" Mimi said. "Just kidding!" She added then, "It's on somebody."

"Who?"

"Somebody."

"Who?"

Mimi folded up the paper and put it in her pocket. "Let's go," she said.

Carrie bent her head over her books as if she was looking for something. But I thought that her bottom lip was shaky, and I could see her swallow hard. It reminded me of Grandma and how she looked last night.

I poked Mimi. "Tell her," I said. "Tell Carrie."

"Why?"

"Just tell her."

Mimi looked at Carrie. "You gonna tell?" she said.

Carrie shook her head no.

"Cross your heart and hope to die?" Mimi said.

Carrie looked up. She didn't look like she was about to cry. "I don't make baby promises," she said. "I said I wouldn't tell, so I won't."

"You're dead if you do," Mimi said.

"I'm real scared," Carrie said.

I was beginning to be sorry that I had made Mimi tell. Carrie was such a pain.

"Okay, it's Munchmore," Mimi said.

Carrie's eyes got wide. "Oooh, you're going to get in trouble."

"No, I'm not, because nobody's going to know, right?" Mimi said. She made a face at Carrie then, and then the whole bunch of us started for school.

As we were walking, Mimi said to me, "Notice I didn't put Munchmore's name in the note—only put 'you-know-who'? That's because he has this weird way of finding notes that are being passed around. It's like he has a secret radar. So if he finds this one, know what I'm going to tell him?"

"What?"

"That we're thinking up April Fools' jokes. Not to do, just for ideas. He can't punish you for just thinking things."

"Bet," I said. "If he's as mean as you say he is."

"He is!" Mimi said. "But he can't get away with that. We have him first period today. He takes over homeroom for Miss Gladstone on Thursday. Wait'll you see him."

We all went into school together and pounded up the stairs. The steps are metal, and everybody tries to make as much noise as possible. Sometimes Miss Tuller comes out of her office and makes us all go down again, but she didn't this day.

On our way up the steps, I said to Mimi, "You know about them maybe tearing down Grandpa's house?"

"Yeah?"

"They might really do it."

"You sure?"

"Not sure. Grandpa says he's working on stopping it."

"Hey, maybe we could do something, too," Mimi said.

"That's what I was thinking. Any ideas?"

But Mimi didn't answer me because we were already at the door of the classroom. She put a hand in front of me, and said, "Now, wait." She was laughing, and she held me back until everyone else had gone in. Then, when she had a good clear view of the room, she whispered, "Come here. Look."

It must have been Munchmore standing there, but from the back, it looked like a piano dressed up in pants and a sweater. I'd never seen anybody that big. I just stared and stared. I must have looked funny, because Mimi started to laugh. She laughed so hard that she got hiccups. And she doesn't just get hiccups like a normal person—she hiccups about a thousand times in a row, real loud.

Munchmore turned around then and I could see

his face. He looked like a Cabbage Patch doll! His whole head was perfectly round, and huge. All but his eyes. They were little and piggy-looking.

The piggy eyes were looking out in the hallway at Mimi and me. Mimi was still hiccuping like a maniac. She pushed me toward the classroom door, and then she fled down the hall to the water fountain.

It was really hard to keep a straight face, but I went in the classroom and walked right up to Munchmore's desk. I gave him the paper Miss Tuller had given to me.

"So, you're Jeremy Martin," he said. I stared at him again. His voice was really nice, friendly and soft, not at all what I'd have expected from someone his size. Not that I really knew what a piano-size person would sound like, but I guess I expected him to sound big and fat. "You've been here before, I see," he said.

He smiled at me then, and even his smile wasn't so bad. And I didn't smell what Mimi and Libby had said you smelled when you were near him.

"I hear you're a very good student," he said.

I nodded. I never know what to say when people say that to me.

"You like school?" he asked.

Again I nodded.

He frowned, and I realized I should say something. Grandma says that sometimes I act like the cat's got my tongue.

"Uh, yes, sir," I said.

"What's your best subject, Jeremy?"

"Don't know. English, maybe. But I like them all."
I wondered if I should say that I liked music.

"I take it you already have friends in this class,"
he said. "If you'd like to sit beside someone special,
feel free to move the desks around. They're mov-
able . . . but I guess you remember that."

He put the paper I had given him on the desk and
went back to writing on the blackboard.

I walked to where Libby was waiting for me. Mimi
came back from the water fountain at the same time.
The room was unusually quiet, not at all like it
used to be with Miss Gladstone. I found an empty
desk, and pushed it over between Mimi's and Libby's
desks.

"What'd he say?" Mimi whispered.

"He was nice!"

Libby rolled her eyes. "Nice like Dracula," she
muttered.

"He was, though," I said. "Really."

Libby shrugged.

I turned to Mimi. "You know what?" I said. "Maybe
you shouldn't trick him. He seems okay."

And he did. When I looked up at the front of the
room, he was writing my name on the board in curly
letters, introducing me to the class again, probably.

But then he wrote Mimi's and Libby's names under
mine.

"What's he doing?" I asked.

The twins looked up.

"But that's—" Mimi jumped up. "Hey, you can't—"

Munchmore was watching her. "I wouldn't say anything that you'll regret," he said. He held the chalk in his hand, as if daring her to speak.

Mimi sat down again. She banged her desk open and started slamming books and rummaging around inside the desk as though she were looking for something. I knew she was doing it just to make noise.

She said, loud enough for him to hear, "Our names are up there because we were talking in class." She dropped her desk top and it crashed down. "Mr. Mun— Mountmore, that stinks. I'll bet you didn't even tell Jeremy what the class rules are."

Munchmore smiled, and I was reminded of a snakeskin cracking. It wasn't at all like his smile from before. "Judging from her record, and how smart she is, I'd say that Jeremy understands that we don't talk in class. That's a fairly universal rule, isn't it, Miss Martin?"

I just stared at him.

He looked back at me, his eyebrows raised, that snaky smile on his face, as if he were actually waiting for an answer.

"Isn't it, Miss Martin?" he said again.

"No," I said. "No, it's not."

He just shook his head. "Well. So I guess you're not quite as special—as smart—as you think you are."

I never said I was special. Or smart! He's the one who said it! That was so mean!

"So," he said. "I'll expect a four-hundred-word

composition from each of you tomorrow morning."

Again he gave his snaky smile.

Libby was wrong. You could pull tricks on a teacher. The meaner the better. And I knew then that I was going to enter Mimi's contest. I'd come up with the best trick of all. Something he really deserved.

5

Next day, all of us brought in our compositions. I'd done mine about my summer vacation, because I'd written that every September since I'd been in school, and I could practically do it in my sleep. Mimi did one called "What I Dreamed Last Night," about this huge beast who sounded an awful lot like Munchmore. Mimi said since it was a dream, he couldn't really get mad. Libby did one about her favorite pet turtle that she didn't have.

We gave the compositions to Munchmore, but he didn't even read them. He just set them on the corner of Miss Gladstone's desk, and later, after music was over and he was gone, I noticed that they were still there. So when Miss Gladstone wasn't looking, I slid mine quietly off the desk, to keep in case I needed it some other time. When I told Mimi and Libby at recess time, they broke up laughing. Later, when we all went back into the classroom, the twins stole back their compositions, too. If Munchmore started looking for them, that was his problem. We had turned them in. We couldn't help it if they got lost.

For the next couple days, school was definitely fun. I didn't even think about S.B. or about Grandpa's house the whole time I was at school. So much was going on, it was easy to forget for a while.

The best thing was the contest for tricks to pull on Munchmore. I had completely gotten over my feeling that this wasn't a nice thing to do. He wasn't nice, so why should we be? For instance, Julia didn't bring in her recorder one day because it still had the smell of throw-up on it, and she was airing it out. Munchmore made her sit on a chair in the front of the room facing the blackboard for the whole music period, like she was some kind of baby. That did it. Everybody came up with ideas.

Mimi gets really weird sometimes, and this was one of the times. She wouldn't take anyone's idea unless it was given to her during Math. That meant that for forty-five minutes, there was this constant parade of people going to the pencil sharpener, or to get a tissue off Miss Gladstone's desk, or something so they could drop their notes onto Mimi's lap on the way.

Of course, Miss Gladstone finally caught on. One day she announced, "Class, we're going to make a real effort to stay in our seats today. No one is to get up without permission." So we knew she knew, because she's not the kind of teacher who makes you ask every time you have to go to the bathroom or something.

That day it was raining, so after lunch, instead of going out to the playground, we came back to our classroom for indoor recess. On rainy days, Miss Steinborn, the lunch monitor, comes in and unlocks the supply closet, and we're each allowed to choose a game.

Miss Steinborn is real tall and skinny, with frizzed yellow hair that sticks out all around so that she looks like some kind of dandelion. The only thing not skinny about her is her chest. That's huge. She wears lime-green polyester pantsuits, with the creases sewn down the front of the legs, and there's always a grease stain on her jacket where her boobs stick out. All the boys joke about it, Michael especially. He says it's so big it should be called the "community chest." But the worst thing about Steinborn is her mouth. She really shouts. She could go in the *Guinness Book of World Records* for her shouting.

That day, Steinborn stood there with her arms folded while we chose our games, and when we were finished and had sat down, she locked the closet back up. She went on to the next room, but before she left, she shouted, "Behave!"

As soon as she was gone, Mimi got up and closed the door. "I have all the Munchmore tricks here," she said. "Everybody listen." She pulled out her math book and took out the notes that everyone had been passing to her.

Right away, we all bunched up around her desk. All but weird Andrew. He stayed at his desk by the window, laying out a game of solitaire. Jay Clutter sat down at a desk behind Andrew, probably to think up some trouble. He's always tormenting Andrew.

"Read mine, read mine," Robert Roda said.

"Read mine, mine's best!" Michael shouted. He elbowed his way in so he was closest to Mimi's desk. "I say we put a whoopee cushion on his chair!"

"I'm reading these," Mimi said. She glared at Michael. She used to say she was in love with him, but now she says she hates him. I'm not sure which is true. Some days she's really friendly to him, and some days she won't even speak to him.

"What's a whoopee cushion?" somebody said.

"Find mine, mine's best!" Jay Clutter shouted from over by the window. He was folding paper planes, preparing to hurl them at the back of Andrew's head.

"Everybody knows what a whoopee cushion is," Robert Roda said, in his best stuck-up voice.

"I don't," Carrie piped up.

"You wouldn't," Mimi said.

"It's a cushion that, when you sit on it, it makes a sound like you let out a big one," Robert said, like he was doing everyone a big favor by explaining it.

"Only there's no smell," Michael added.

"Imagine if he really did let one loose?" Iris said in her super-soft voice.

Everyone screamed.

"He's the type who farts and blames it on the dog, you can tell," Libby said.

"Yeah, a dog!" Jay Carson said. "We could get dog poop and put it in his car!" He started dancing around Mimi's desk, hopping from one foot to the other, like he was trying to wipe dog stuff off his feet.

There was a lot of noise by then, and Mimi said, "Will you all please . . . *shut . . . up?*" She really shouted the "shut up" part.

"Listen to her shout!" Mark said. "She thinks she's Steinborn."

That really made everybody scream.

Mimi snapped her math book shut on the notes.

"All right, all right, everybody," Michael said. "Be quiet." He held out his hands, and the room got as quiet as if Steinborn had come in.

"Okay," Mimi said. She opened the book again. "You heard Michael's. Bruce Mueller says we should hide the chalk."

A bunch of people groaned, but quietly.

"Boring!" Jennifer said.

"Not!" Bruce said. His ears got red. "You know how he loves to fill in quarter notes on the blackboard. He takes up a whole period filling in quarter notes."

"Boring!" a whole bunch of other people said.

Mimi read from another note. "This is Mark's. 'Pick one of the stupid songs that he makes us play all the time—like "This Land Is Your Land"—and everybody swear that we can't play it because he never taught it to us.' "

"Boring! Boring, boring, boring!" A chant started. "Let's hear something not so boring," Michael shouted.

" 'Rattlesnake eggs,' " Mimi read. "That's Libby's."

Rattlesnake eggs are those things you make from a paper clip or a bobby pin and a rubber band, and put in an envelope. When the person opens the envelope, the rubber band unwinds and spins the clip, making a noise. It usually scares the wits out of the person for a second.

"Boring! Boring, boring, boring." Robert Roda and Michael and the other Jay wound their arms around each other's shoulders and began chanting it together. I guess Michael figured that if he said it enough, he'd get to do the whoopee cushion thing. Joy, who is a big flirt just like Michael, got in the circle with the boys and began singing it, too. "Boring! Boring, boring, boring!"

"I've got one, I've got one!" Jennifer shouted over the chanting. "How about this—we stick a sign on his back that says, 'Don't speak to me. I am not a person. I am a hippopotamus.' "

A couple of people laughed, but Michael shouted again, "Boring!"

Nobody was even paying attention to Mimi by then. They were all coming up with new ideas.

"A Chinese fire drill!" Julia said. "You know, where everybody gets up and changes seats at the same time?"

"Yeah, during the Iowa Tests!" Robert yelled.

But Munchmore's not even in the room when we're taking the Iowa Tests. And besides, I had the best idea, and I wanted to make sure they heard it. I jumped on a desk chair. "Listen to mine!" I shouted.

Michael and Jay and Robert and Joy were swaying back and forth as they were chanting, "Boring!" Suddenly, one of them lost his balance, and all four fell over. Robert lay on the floor clutching his stomach.

"Oh, I'm Munchmore, and I've munched too much!" he groaned.

"Listen to mine!" I said.

There was finally some quiet because the "boring" chant had stopped. "Listen," I said in the sudden silence.

Stein—born! Mimi was mouthing something at me, but no sound was coming out of her mouth. *Stein-born*, she mouthed again, and there was no doubt what she was saying.

I slid down into the chair.

Robert and the others scrambled up off the floor.

"You are out of your places!" Steinborn shouted from the doorway. She pointed a long, bony finger at me. "You are out of your place!"

She looked like she expected me to say something. I couldn't think of anything to say.

"And standing on a chair! A chair!" She made it sound like a curse word. "Why?"

She looked like she really expected an answer.

"The hem of her dress was coming loose," Mimi said, "and I was trying to help her fix it. See?" She reached over and pulled at my skirt, yanking it up for Miss Steinborn to see.

I pulled it back down. Everybody could see my underwear if she made it go any higher.

But Mimi didn't let go. "See?" she said. "You have to get up on a chair to fix a hem. My mother always—"

"That's enough, Mimi," Miss Steinborn said. But she seemed to have calmed down a little. "If I hear another sound from this room, you will all fold your arms on your desks and put your heads down for the rest of your free period. *Is* that clear?"

Nobody answered.

"Is that clear?" she repeated.

Her voice was rising, and we could just feel her warming up to shout again, so everybody said, "Yes, Miss Steinborn." She took a deep breath, and her huge chest rose up and settled down again. I didn't dare look at Michael.

"That's better," she said. She went out in the hall again. "And don't shut this door!" she bellowed from the doorway.

For a minute, we were real quiet, and then Julia tiptoed over to the door, peeped out and said, "She's gone."

"That was close," I said to Mimi.

She grinned.

"What was your idea?" Michael said, and he smiled at me. He's a big flirt, and he thinks all the girls are in love with him. Some of them are, but not me.

I looked at Julia. She was still by the door. She nodded at me that it was safe.

"Okay," I said. "You know how Munchmore always takes off his jacket and puts on his smelly sweater—the one he keeps in the coat closet—the minute he comes in? And how he sticks his hands way deep in his pockets?"

"He thinks he's Mr. Rogers," Michael said.

"Only Mr. Rogers doesn't stick his hands in his pockets," Jay said.

"Listen!" I said. "So we take his sweater from the coat closet after school, take it home—"

"And throw it away!" Michael yelled. "Then it won't stink up our coats anymore."

"Would you guys shut up and listen?" I said.

"Yich!" Jennifer said. She held her nose with one hand. The other hand she stretched out in front of her, two fingers pinched together like she was holding Munchmore's sweater.

"And then," I said. "We sew up the pockets. Real tight. Then next day, we watch him trying to get his hands—"

"Oh, yeah! Yeah, yeah!" Everybody began yelling at once again.

"Boring!" one person said, but nobody took up the chant.

"Yeah, and we sew a lizard inside the pocket!" Robert yelled.

"A mouse!" somebody said.

"Chewed-up bubble gum."

"Dog poop."

"Rattlesnake eggs."

Everybody was screaming again.

"No, no, I got it!" Joy was trying to get a word in.

"No!" Mimi yelled. "Just plain. Just plain sew up the pockets."

"Can't you just see the look on his face?" Libby said.

"Okay, Jeremy," Michael shouted. "It's your idea. You do it!"

There was too much noise. It was bound to happen. Julia came diving toward her seat, and there wasn't a sound by the time Steinborn came barreling through the doorway. But she still made us fold our arms on our desks and put our heads down like we were a bunch of kindergarten babies. It got real quiet in the room and stayed that way because Steinborn stayed in the doorway.

While I had my head down, I kept wondering if I'd really be brave enough to steal the sweater from the coat closet. And if I did, where and when could I do the sewing without Grandma knowing? It was a great idea, and I couldn't wait to see the look on Munchmore's face if I really did do it. I was worried, too, though. What if he found out it was me? I mean I knew he couldn't. But just suppose he did?

6

I was beginning to think I was going to suffocate with my head down on my arms like that, when finally Miss Gladstone came and let us up.

Miss Gladstone is about six feet tall, and she has a voice sort of like a cartoon animal. But she's nice to us, and everybody knows she likes kids and likes being a teacher. When she heard about the noise, she only said, "Really, class," but you could tell she wasn't that upset. One, I don't think she minds noise the way other grown-ups do. And two, I think she hates Miss Steinborn as much as the rest of us do. One day out on the playground, Miss Steinborn was yelling at some little kid, and Miss Gladstone was watching her. After a while, Miss Gladstone shook her head, and I heard her mutter under her breath, "Bitch." When Miss Gladstone saw me watching her, she shook her head again and said, "Boy!" But I know what she really said.

That afternoon, after she let us sit up, she said, "Boys and girls, take out a piece of paper and a pencil. Today we'll be beginning a new project."

Project?

Right away, Mimi groaned, right out loud.

I groaned, too, but not out loud. Projects stink. Last year, I did six dioramas. In one year!

Miss Gladstone frowned at Mimi, then went on, "We'll begin a project on the fifty states. You can pick any state you wish. Choose one of these items: discoverers and explorers, or historic monuments and buildings. . . ."

I looked at Mimi. She opened her mouth and stuck one finger up in front of it like she was gagging.

I nodded and did the same thing with two fingers.

Miss Gladstone was going on about how we were to do a report on the state—no dioramas!—and when it was due and all that boring stuff, so I just tuned her out. I'd catch up on the details later.

With my pencil, I began making little dots on a notebook page, making up my own game of connect-the-dots.

Mimi tore off a piece of paper, wrote something on it, and passed it to me below desk level.

It said, "I just saw Carrie pick her nose, look at the stuff, and flick it away. Let's collect the buggers from the floor around her desk and put them in Munchmore's pockets."

"Can't," I wrote back. "There aren't enough. Half the time she eats them."

"Miss Gladstone, Miss Gladstone!" Everyone was shouting at once.

What had I missed?

I poked Libby. "What's happening?" I said it right out loud because there was so much noise, anyway.

"A prize," Libby said. "She's going to give a prize for the best report."

"What kind of prize?"

That's what everybody else was trying to find out. That and about a hundred other things.

"What prize, Miss Gladstone?"

"What state, Miss Gladstone?"

"Miss Gladstone, can I choose New York?"

About fifteen people wanted to do New York. There's fifteen kids in the class.

But I wanted to know about the prize. "What's the prize, Miss Gladstone?" I said, louder than anybody else.

"The prize will be kept a secret," she answered.

That was pretty dirty. What was the good of working really hard for a prize, if it turned out to be a gift certificate at a health food store or something?

Mimi had already pulled out her notebook, and I could see her writing in big letters across the top of a page: ALASKA. Knowing her, she'd have her report finished before anyone else even started. She didn't look things up in the reference books or anything. She just made it up out of her head, but it always sounded good. Like last fall, when we had to write about what we did on our summer vacation, Mimi had written that she'd gone to Alaska even though she'd never left Brooklyn all summer.

"Boys and girls!" Miss Gladstone said it severely, and everybody settled down. "You can start with the reference books—the World Books, the other encyclopedias. Just remember that two people can't do the same state, so it might be a good idea to consult with your neighbors."

Everybody started talking again. Bruce yelled loudest, so he got New York. Besides, he's teacher's pet. But then other big arguments broke out. All the boys wanted Texas. And all the girls wanted California.

Mimi, Libby, and I pushed our desks together.

"I'm doing Alaska," Mimi said.

"I'm doing Montana," Libby said. "It's square. I like square states."

"You're weird," Mimi said.

"I'm doing Rhode Island," I said. "It's the smallest state. That way, if Miss Gladstone says my report's too short, I'll just tell her there's not that much to say about a small state."

I got up then and went to get the encyclopedias. But the "R" books were missing, and I could see Jay Clutter with them, copying from them into his notebook, word for word. He covered his paper with his arm when he saw me looking.

So I decided on the second smallest state—Connecticut. I got this great picture in my mind about Munchmore moving to the tiny state of Connecticut. The minute he stepped inside the state, he weighed it all down so it fell right into Long Island Sound.

And if he went there today, or even if he went to Montana, I wouldn't have to do anything about the sweater. I wouldn't admit it to anybody, but I was scared about what we were going to do.

That afternoon, when class was dismissed and we were sent row-by-row to the coat closet to get our things, I could feel everybody in class watching me. I wondered if Miss Gladstone noticed. This was when I had to do it. My heart was just racing. If Mimi had come to the coat closet with me I probably wouldn't have been so scared, but because she sat next to me, her row went after mine.

I went in the closet and got my coat. But I couldn't bring myself to touch the smelly black sweater. I just looked at it, hanging on the hook right there inside the closet door.

The two Jays were already in the coat closet, and Jay Clutter grinned at me. He grabbed the sweater and flung it toward me. "Catch!" he said.

I ducked, or it would have draped right over my head. "You absolute jerk!" I said. I glared at him. But now I had to do it. I put my coat down and picked the sweater up off the floor with just two fingers. I dropped the sweater on my coat, then folded my coat over and then up, like I was making a package of it. And prayed that Miss Gladstone wouldn't tell me to put my coat on when it was time to leave.

"Gonna be ready tomorrow?" Jay Carson said.

I shrugged. "Maybe. I have to be sure I have the right color thread." I didn't want to admit how scared I was. That I might try to put it off.

"*Black?*" he said. "Everybody's got black thread."

"Boys and girls?" It was Miss Gladstone. "There are others waiting."

We went out of the closet, and the next row was sent in. "You got it?" Mimi said to me real quietly as she went by.

I nodded.

"Where?"

I looked down at my coat.

I went and sat down, but my heart was absolutely pounding. I couldn't imagine how anybody could be a thief or a shoplifter. I was just terrified. I felt as if my coat were see-through, and Miss Gladstone and everybody else could tell what was in there. People kept walking by my desk and smiling at me. Every time I looked up, Michael winked. I pretended not to notice any of them.

When the bell rang, first the busers were dismissed and then the walkers. Since practically everybody is a walker, there was a bunch of us who went out together. I was almost through the doorway when Miss Gladstone called to me. "Jeremy! It's cold out there. Put your coat on."

"I will!" I said, but I didn't stop.

In the hall, Mimi, Libby, and I headed straight for the stairs. We didn't run, just fastwalked, so nobody would stop us. When we got to the steps, we didn't pound on them, but raced down as quietly as we could. I hardly dared to breathe. By the time we got to the downstairs hall, we were running.

We burst through the front door. Outside. Safe!

I finally started breathing again. And shivering,

too. It *was* cold out there. I shook out my coat, and the sweater fell out. Mimi picked it up while I put my coat on.

"Buy your suits from the Big and Tall Man Shops!" she said in this big, deep voice, like she was a radio announcer. She held the sweater up in front of her.

"Will you shush?" I said, looking around. "And hide that!" We had raced out so fast that none of the kids were there yet, and the teachers never come outside anyway. But still, she shouldn't have been holding it up like that.

"You worry too much," Mimi said. But she rolled the sweater up and stuffed it into her backpack.

I saw Carrie coming down the school steps. "Let's go," I said.

"Our house," Libby said. "Nobody's home, and we can do it."

We started toward the twins' house.

While we were walking, Mimi said, "You know how Carrie and Michael are in the coat closet the same time as me? Well, when we were in there, Michael and me were laughing about the sweater, and Carrie goes, 'I don't think you should do that.' And so I go, 'Who asked you?' And she goes, 'It's very *immicha*.' "

"Very what?" Libby said.

"Immature. But that's how she says it—'immicha.' "

"She's immature," I said.

"Yeah, that's what Michael said. He goes, 'You're immicha, Carrie,' and he looks right at her chest."

Mimi laughed when she said it, and I did, too. But Libby said, "Michael's disgusting."

"He's funny sometimes," Mimi said. "Anyway, Carrie's just a scaredy cat. But I can't wait till tomorrow. Can't you just picture Munchmore?"

"I guess." But I couldn't feel as excited as they seemed to be. I was really scared. Maybe as scared as Carrie. I'd never done anything like this to a teacher. How come Mimi and Libby didn't get scared the way I did?

Mimi was looking at me. "What's the matter?" she said.

I shrugged. Mimi used to call me a chicken last year, and it made me really mad. "Nothing," I said.

"I'll keep the sweater overnight and put it back tomorrow, if you want," Mimi said.

I looked at her. "Yeah?" I said.

"Yeah." She didn't say it like she was making fun of me or anything. "I don't mind."

"Okay, then," I said, and I felt relieved. Because that was one of the scariest parts of what we were doing, just having the sweater in my hands and sneaking it in and out of school.

"Can't wait," Mimi said.

"Can't wait!" Libby said.

"Me neither," I said. This time I meant it. Now that we had gotten around the corner from school, and now that Mimi was going to take the sweater back, it was beginning to seem like fun again. I just couldn't wait to see the look on Munchmore's face when he tried to jam his hands into his pockets. Pockets that weren't there anymore.

7

Libby was right. There was nobody home at the twins' house, and it was easy to get thread and sew the pockets up tight. We were hysterical, laughing the whole time, just thinking how it was going to be next day when Munchmore tried to put his hands in his pockets. We knew he'd get mad and try to find out who had done it, but since everybody was in on the trick, no one would tell. Even *immicha* Carrie had promised not to tell.

"He can't punish a whole class," I said.

"I'm going to tell him that it was probably another teacher who did it," Mimi said.

"Yeah?" Libby said. "Good idea. He'll believe it." She was making tiny, baby stitches along the top of the sweater pocket, so small you could hardly see them. "And you know why?" she said. "I'll bet the other teachers don't like him any more than they like Steinborn. He and Steinborn should get married."

"And have a baby," Mimi said. "Then they could be the Munch Bunch."

"Yeah," Libby said, "and the baby could be—"

"A Munchkin!" I said. "It would probably come out weighing sixty pounds. A sixty-pound Munchkin."

We were taking turns sewing the pockets. The only problem was, the sweater stank so bad that while we sewed, we kept taking turns sticking our heads out of the window so we could breathe fresh air.

When we were finished, Mimi rolled the sweater up and put it in her backpack. "I can't wait till tomorrow to see his face," she said.

I had to go home then, and I was glad to leave the sweater there with the twins. "See you tomorrow," I said.

When I got home, instead of going upstairs right away, I stopped in the store to see Grandpa. He was talking with a customer when I came in—a bald guy with a super-shiny head—but when he saw me, he excused himself and came right over. He put a hand on my shoulder.

"How's . . . things?" he said, and he smiled.

I knew he'd been about to say, "How's school?" But I've told him a thousand times that there's only one answer to that: boring. Except for the parts like jokes on Munchmore, but those I didn't tell about. Not always, anyway.

"Pretty good," I said. "Look at this." I showed him the map I'd already done for my state project. I'm really great at freehand drawing. I don't even have to use tracing paper. I'd drawn Connecticut, and in it I'd put all the boring facts that Miss Gladstone expected: 5,009 square miles in area; one of the original thirteen states; capital, Hartford; Connecticut River flows through it, largest river in New England, blah, blah, blah.

With his finger, Grandpa traced the outline of the map. "Nice work," he said. He didn't mean the written stuff, but the important part, the drawing.

"Thank you," I said.

"Want to go to Connecticut someday? There's lots of history there," he said.

"With you?"

"With me."

"Sure." I smiled at him.

He smiled back. Then he held out a little paint card that he had in his hand. "Would you mind getting a gallon of this color paint from the basement storage room for me?" he said. "Young legs are better on stairs than old ones."

"You're not old," I said. I hate it when he says that.

"Old enough," he said.

"Old enough to what?" I asked. I didn't look at him. Ever since Grandma said that night that he'd die if he retired, I've been thinking about it a lot. I wanted to ask him if old people really did die when they retired. But even though he was the one who usually answered my questions, this was one question I was pretty sure I shouldn't ask.

He just laughed.

The bald guy was clearing his throat.

Grandpa winked at me and went back to the counter where the baldie was waiting. The guy had the roundest, shiniest head I'd ever seen, with big knobs that stuck out on the back of it. Like a bowling ball with handles.

I went out the door into the little hallway, and then down the steps to the basement storage room where Grandpa keeps the odd-colored paints. I flicked on the light down there. It's the spookiest place in the world. It's not like ordinary basements. Part of it has a regular concrete floor. But then you go back and down a few steps, and there's another part that has a dirt floor. The part that's dirt has wooden walls that were cut right from tree trunks. You can even see some of the bark still on the trees. But it stinks down there, all moldy, and it feels dark even with the lights on, so I always hurry when I'm down there. I saw the rows of paint cans on the wall shelves, arranged from pale colors to dark. I quick found the one he wanted—pink—bright pink. Poinsettia pink, it said on the label and on the matching card. I ran back up the stairs with a can of it in my hand. The can was pretty heavy. Dusty, too. I set it down on the counter, and Grandpa smiled at me.

When Grandpa had finished with his customer, he

came back over to me. "Thanks for getting the paint for me," he said. "Now you better scoot upstairs to your grandma because—Oh, there she is."

He nodded toward the door of the store. Through the window part, we could see Grandma just about to come in. "She has some news for you," he said.

I stopped dead still. "What?" I said.

He didn't answer right away. He just put a hand on my shoulder. "Let her tell you," he said.

I didn't say anything.

I just watched Grandma come in. I knew what her news was going to be. S.B. I'd bet anything. I didn't want to hear it. I didn't want to hear one single thing about Stupid Baby.

The minute Grandma saw me, she said, "Where have you been? I was beginning to worry."

"I'm sorry," I said. "I was at the twins'. I forgot to call."

"It's all right. I thought that's where you were." She smiled at me. "I have something for you." She reached in the pocket of her apron, brought out a letter, and handed it to me. From Mom! I recognized the handwriting, and the airmail envelope with the funny stamps. So it wasn't about S.B. It was just a letter, because Mom had said if they actually got a baby, she'd call, not write.

I sat down on the big stool that Grandpa keeps there at the counter and tore open the letter. I was so happy. I'd really missed Mom.

"Dear Jeremy," I read silently to myself. "We miss you, darling. Daddy and I really miss you. I hope you're having fun with all your friends. What we're doing isn't exactly *fun*, but it is rewarding. Because—guess what? Our dearest dream seems to be about to come true. How would you like a tiny baby sister? . . ."

Their dearest dream—a baby sister! Is that what their dearest dream was? What about me? I looked up from the letter.

Grandma was watching me, a sort of expectant happy look on her face like she was about to burst into a laugh. "I got a letter, too," she said when she saw me look up. "Isn't it wonderful? Aren't you excited?"

I shrugged. "I haven't finished it yet," I said, and I bent my head over the letter again so she couldn't see my face.

". . . Her name is Nichole," Mom's letter went on. "She's half Colombian and half American, with dark hair and dark eyes. And she's just beautiful. We were going to change her name and name her ourselves, but isn't Nichole a pretty name? And somehow, it seems to suit her perfectly. I can't wait till you see her. There are loads of things yet to be done—shots and things to have, papers to be signed. She's not really ours yet. So it may be a while before we can come home. And she's tiny, Jeremy—so very, very tiny—that we have to be sure she's strong enough before we travel with her. But she is well, honey. We're almost certain of that, even though she's so small. She's just perfect. . . ."

I looked up again. Grandma had begun dusting

the upper shelves with that long duster thing she keeps in the store, and she was humming to herself. Grandpa was standing right where he'd been before when Grandma first came in the store. He was watching me now, his eyebrows raised, that look on his face that he always gets when he wants to know what I'm thinking. When he saw me looking at him, he leaned his head toward me like he was listening to me, even though I hadn't said anything.

I looked down and read the letter again. ". . . And, oh, honey, Nichole is so beautiful. Almost as beautiful as you were when you were a baby. . . ."

Sure. Almost as pretty as me! Throw that in so I wouldn't be jealous.

". . . Daddy and I hope school is going well for you and that you're happy. And I just know that you're having fun with your friends. Are you feeling all right? You are taking your medicine, aren't you? We'll call you in a few days—the beginning of next week so I can actually hear your voice. Meanwhile, let's think about doing something different this summer—maybe having the twins spend the summer with you at our house for a change? We'll talk about it soon, all right? I miss you, love. Baby Bear misses you, too. Love, Mom."

For a long time after I had finished the letter, I kept my head bent over it, pretending I was still reading it. Mom was just bribing me, talking about having the twins spend the summer at my house. When all I wanted was for her to leave the baby there and come home. But it was stupid to be jealous.

It was only a baby. And Mom would play at pretending she was Baby Bear for Baby Nichole—just the way she used to do it for me, leaving little presents and notes from Baby Bear. Only now, she wouldn't do it for me anymore.

I stood up. Grandpa was still there watching me, that questioning look on his face. I wanted to tear up the letter, but I couldn't with him looking at me like that. So instead I just stuck it inside my notebook.

Grandma turned from her dusting. "So," she said brightly. "What do you think?"

"I think I'll go do my homework," I said.

8

When Grandpa came up for supper that night, I wondered if he was going to say anything about the baby. I didn't want him to talk about it—not at all. It was bad enough listening to Grandma, but somehow I couldn't stand the thought of him doing it, too. Talking about it made it more real. That's why I hadn't told the twins yet, even though a part of me wanted to tell them. So far, Grandpa hadn't said a word about it. Which was just fine with me.

We sat down to eat, but I didn't feel like having dinner at all. I felt so alone, like I had no one to talk to. Usually I can talk to Grandpa, but this I couldn't tell him. I'd sound stupid and jealous and mean, too. Besides, I'd probably blurt out the question I couldn't ask, that was too stupid to ask—if I were really special, really important, why did Mom and Dad have to go get another kid? Grandma and Grandpa had only had one. Why did Mom and Daddy need two?

All through supper, I barely said anything. And since Grandpa is usually quiet anyway, that gave Grandma a chance to talk nonstop. Which is what she loves. She talked a lot about Mom and Daddy, but she didn't say much about S.B. I wondered if that meant that she knew—at least a little bit—how I felt.

When supper was just about over, Grandpa lit up his pipe and looked at Grandma. "Mr. Lawlor was in the store today," he said.

"Oh?" Grandma said.

"Who's Mr. Lawlor?" I said, looking from one of them to the other. "The bald guy?"

Grandpa spoke directly to Grandma. "He thinks if the Citizens' Committee doesn't come up with something new to stop this highway, and pretty quick, too, all the permits will be signed."

There was a long silence, and Grandma said, "And then what?"

Grandpa just looked at her.

For another long minute, Grandma didn't speak. Then she said quietly, "It will be too late—if it's not already."

Grandpa nodded.

"Too late for what?" I asked.

Nobody answered me.

"You mean they'll tear down your house?" I asked.

Grandma sighed. "After all these years," she said. "And there's nothing new we can hope for?"

Grandpa poked around in his pipe with this little metal thing, but the whole time he didn't take his eyes off Grandma. "The historical angle," he said. "But that's hard to discover. Harder to prove. And it takes time. Other than that . . ." He put the pipe back in his mouth.

"If it's historical," I said, "does that mean they can't tear it down?"

I waited for an answer, looking from one of them to the other. "Would somebody mind talking to *me?*" I said at last.

This long look was going between Grandma and Grandpa, and it was one of those private kinds of looks, like Grandpa gives me so often. This time, though, it didn't include me.

I stood up. "I'm going to go watch TV," I said.

I started to leave the room but I took my time, waiting to see if they would say anything. Grandma always tells me that I have to do my homework first. Grandpa always gives me that secret smile or wink that he gives only to me. But Grandma didn't say anything, and Grandpa didn't even look at me. He probably didn't even notice that I left.

I guess I must have fallen asleep in front of the TV, because next thing I knew, Grandpa was leaning over me. "Time for bed," he said softly.

"It's stupid to wake up to go to sleep," I muttered.

"Can't sleep in your clothes."

"Can." But I struggled to sit up.

Grandpa sat down next to me on the sofa. He reached over and took one of the pipes he keeps on the table there. He must have about a thousand pipes in different places around the house. He spent a long time lighting it. After he had it going and had puffed on it for a while, he said quietly, "Anything you want to talk about?" He was looking straight ahead, as if he was watching the TV.

"Like what?" I asked.

He didn't answer.

"No," I said.

"It's going to be all right, you know," he said.

I didn't know if he meant the house or Stupid Baby. But how could he say that? Neither of them was going to be all right.

"Huh!" I said. I turned my face away from him.

"You do love coming here, don't you?" Grandpa said.

I nodded. I was suddenly too close to tears to speak.

"It won't be the same," Grandpa said. "I know that, but—"

"You *don't* know!" I said. "You don't know any-thing."

He didn't answer for a minute, and then he said, "Then why don't you tell me?"

I hesitated. "You're going to die if you move away from here!" I blurted out. And then really started to cry. I hadn't even known I'd been thinking about it right then. But it had been making me scared ever since Grandma said it.

"I am?" Grandpa said.

"Uh-huh. Grandma said so."

"She did?"

"Yes! She said you'd die if you retired. Remember?"

"Oh, that." Grandpa paused. "Jeremy, I'm not planning on dying."

"But you might."

"Anybody might. But I'm not going to."

"Even if you retire?"

"Even if I retire."

"Promise?"

"As far as I know."

I took a deep breath.

"What else, Jeremy?" Grandpa said. "I thought it was the house you were upset about."

"I am," I said. "Because I want a place *here*. In this house. With you!" I wiped my face on the bottom of my sweatshirt.

Grandpa handed me his handkerchief. It was folded and clean and white. I wondered if grown-ups ever cried.

"Jeremy," Grandpa said after a minute. "You'll always have a special place. And no highway authorities or demolition crews—" he smiled—"or even new babies can take it away from you."

"Then what—where—is my place?" I asked.

Grandpa reached out and pulled me close to him. And then he said quietly, "A special place—a place where you belong—isn't always something you can see."

I dreamed that night about an old house. I kept reaching out to touch it, but when I did, it would fade away and be gone. It was dark, but behind me, I could hear Grandpa's voice talking to me, calm and quiet. Yet he spoke in a language that was strange to me, one I didn't understand.

9

And then Grandma was talking to me, saying the same thing over and over again. I opened my eyes, and it wasn't a dream anymore. It really was Grandma.

"Good morning, sleepyhead," she said. "I've been calling you and calling you. Time to get up."

I jumped up, dressed, and then hurried through breakfast. I had to talk to Mimi and Libby. An idea had come to me during the night, an idea for saving the house. Maybe it came in the dream. Or maybe it was from what Grandpa had said about trying to prove that the house was historical. I couldn't wait to talk to them about it.

I was rushing for another reason, even more important. This was the morning Mimi was going to bring in Munchmore's sweater—the sweater with the pockets sewn up tight. I couldn't wait to get to school to see what would happen.

I met Mimi and Libby at the corner in our usual place, and the three of us raced to school together. All of us were too excited to talk about anything but Munchmore right then. Mimi had the sweater rolled up inside a grocery bag. A good place for it. It looked like a big lunch, just big enough for Munchmore, the electric pig.

"I can't wait," Libby said. "But how are we ever going to keep a straight face?"

"I know how," I said. "It works sometimes. I pretend something sad happened—like that my mother died."

"Really?" Mimi said. "Me, too. Only I pretend Libby's dead."

"Gee, thanks!" Libby said.

"Don't get all huffy," Mimi said. "At least it makes me sad."

When we got in the classroom, everybody was waiting to see the sweater. In our class, it's easy to hang around in the coat closet in the mornings, because Miss Gladstone is always busy collecting lunch money or milk money or something. People go in the coat closet and trade lunches and copy homework and everything, and she doesn't even know.

That morning, Mimi put the sweater back on the hook, just normal like, when she hung up her coat. Before she could even turn around, Jennifer and Joy and Michael and Bruce and Robert and the two Jays came cramming into the coat closet. That meant, with Mimi and Libby and me in there, there was practically nobody left in the classroom.

"Let's see!" Michael said.

He grabbed for the sweater, but Mimi grabbed, too, and so did Jay.

Jay won.

"Give it!" Mimi said. She yanked it out of Jay's hands.

Jay fell over backward against the wall, just missing splitting his head open on one of the coat hooks that stick out.

"Dummy!" he said. "Big jerk!"

"Boys and girls!" Miss Gladstone sounded mad.

We shut up in a hurry. Mimi put the sweater on the hook, and we all raced out of the closet.

It seemed like ten-thirty and music period would never come. I was excited, but I was nervous, too. Nobody else seemed nervous at all, except Carrie, who looked like she was about to upchuck any minute. I'll bet she'd never done anything in her entire boring life that she wasn't supposed to do.

Finally, though, it was ten-thirty, and Miss Gladstone gathered up her papers and picked up her thermos. "Mr. Mountmore will be here in a moment," she said. "Enjoy your music period." And she left.

Munchmore was coming. You could always feel him coming before you saw him. The floor shook like a dinosaur was coming down the halls of the school.

Already I could feel myself beginning to want to

laugh, that kind of feeling I got that time in church when the choir director's robe was caught up in his behind, and I knew I'd get in big trouble if I laughed, but I had to anyway.

I wasn't the only one, either. Libby's face was bright red, and Mimi was pinching her lips together with her fingers and there were tears in her eyes. I wondered if she was picturing Libby dead.

"Good morning, good morning," Munchmore said as he came in the classroom, his voice booming in that hearty way he uses before he goes back to his real personality. He looked over the classroom. "You're unusually well-behaved today. Well, who wants to choose the song today?"

He always asks that question as if he really does want a volunteer, but then even if you do offer, he picks the song he wants anyway.

He began to unbutton his huge jacket, and he stepped into the coat closet for the sweater.

Libby's face turned purple.

I didn't dare look at Mimi. It was so quiet in the classroom it was spooky.

"How about 'Popcorn Popping on the Apricot Tree'?" Jay said. He said "apricot" the way Munchmore did— *ayuh-pricot*.

At least that gave us an excuse to laugh—quietly, anyway, and then I was able to breathe again.

Munchmore's huge back was filling the doorway of the coat closet as he shrugged out of his jacket and into his sweater.

Carrie's face was so white it looked like the chalkboard after an eraser fight.

"Well," Munchmore said. He came out of the closet, all dressed up in his sweater. "Take out your recorders and let's get tuned up. I think we'll do 'This Land Is Your Land' today."

Why did he bother to ask?

He took out his own recorder and blew into it, his nostrils puffing out big and dark so they looked like the twin entrances to the Holland Tunnel. Except that the Holland Tunnel doesn't have hairs sticking out of it. We all took out our recorders and tried to match the note he was blowing. We made some really awful sounds. After a minute, he took the recorder out of his mouth, wiped the spit off it, and set it on the desk.

"So," he said, "who would like to try first?"

There were no volunteers. I couldn't keep my eyes off his hands, now that he had put his recorder down.

"Miss Martin," he said. He nodded at me.

"Me?"

"I think that's your name." He gave his snakeskin-cracking smile.

I picked up my recorder and blew one note. My hands were shaking. I took a deep breath and blew again, trying to get the whole first line in one breath. Usually I'm pretty good at it, but this time, I kept feeling as if I was going to laugh, and it was hard to get my lips to stay in the right shape for blowing.

Munchmore strolled down the aisle toward me. This is when he usually did it, his casual, man-walking-on-TV-ad-hands-in-pocket walk.

Oh, God, don't let me laugh.

He was right next to me. He was so close, I could reach out and touch the smelly sweater.

His hands came up and slowly rubbed his huge belly. Then the hands crept down toward the pockets.

I was blowing furiously into the recorder.

Out of the corner of my eye, I watched his stubby fingertips with the chewed cuticles try to slide into the pocket.

They didn't go anywhere. He poked at it. Poked again.

I didn't dare look up to see his face.

I was all the way up to "from California to the New York Island" and still blowing.

I could still see stomach, sweater, and hand out of the corner of my eye. The hand was still fumbling around with the pocket, but scrabbling and scratching as if he was getting annoyed. The stomach seemed to be getting excited, too, puffing up and down furiously the way Miss Steinborn's chest did when she got excited. Then he took a step away from me and I couldn't see him from the side anymore, so I had to look up.

With one hand, he pulled the sweater out away from his side so he could look down into the pocket. With the other hand, he was feeling around the top where the stitches were.

I suddenly realized it was absolutely silent in the room except for my blowing. I kept right on going. "From the redwood forest, to the Gulf stream waters, this land was . . ."

Munchmore frowned, and then started tugging at

the stitches. He got this look on his face like he couldn't believe what he was seeing. Then his big, round face got red, almost purple—like a Cabbage Patch doll about to have a heart attack.

I finished the first verse but I didn't dare stop. I went back to the beginning and started in on the second. I was going really fast by then. "As I was walking that ribbon of highway . . ."

Munchmore looked up. "That . . . is enough," he said in that dangerously soft voice he uses sometimes.

I stopped blowing. "Did I make a mistake?" I asked.

Bold as brass, my grandma would say. I couldn't believe I had said it.

"You did," he said. "Someone did."

There was this long, long silence. Munchmore raised his hand, and wiggled one fat finger at us. "Stay in your places," he said. He was still talking super-quiet. "I will be back in a moment. And someone will regret this childish trick."

He looked absolutely gleeful as he left the room.

10

As soon as he was gone, Carrie threw up. There was just this little burp, and then a splash. Her breakfast sat there in a small pile on the desk in front of her.

Mimi looked at me. "What a neat thrower-upper," she said.

Michael stood up. "I'll get Mr. Jackson," he said.

I jumped up. "I'll do it!" I said. I raced out of the room and down the hall to the janitor's closet before Michael could even move. I had to get out of that classroom. It wasn't the throwup. I was used to that. There's a kid in my other school who throws up every single Monday morning all year long. But I had never played a trick on a teacher before, and I was pretty scared. What if he found out it was us—*me*?

I told Mr. Jackson about Carrie, and he picked up a pail and his mop and that smelly disinfectant and started down the hall to our classroom. I followed him, my heart absolutely racing.

We got there just as Munchmore arrived with Miss Tuller.

Miss Tuller! The principal. Now we were in trouble.

I slid into my seat. I looked at Mimi. Even she didn't seem too happy right then.

Miss Tuller stood in the doorway surveying the classroom. She turned to Iris. "Iris, would you please walk Carrie to the nurse?"

Iris got up, and Carrie did, too. Carrie was kind of wobbly.

"You'll be all right, dear," she said to Carrie as they went out.

"Now," she said. "Who can tell me what this is all about?"

Nobody answered.

Munchmore still looked gleeful.

"Someone?" Miss Tuller prompted.

"Carrie threw up," Mimi said.

Miss Tuller gave her one of those long, silent *looks*. Mimi shut up.

Miss Tuller cleared her throat. "Mr. Mountmore tells me that the pockets of his sweater have been . . ." She paused and did something strange with her mouth. It looked like she was swallowing a burp. "Have been . . ." She had to stop again. "Sewn closed?" she said. Her voice came out kind of weird. Was she trying not to laugh?

Still nobody said anything. Everyone was watching Mr. Jackson scooping up Carrie's breakfast. Miss Tuller looked where we were looking. She kept her head turned that way for a long time, and then she turned back to us again.

"All right," she said. She seemed to have her voice under control again. "Since no one is willing to talk about it, then you may all stay after school tomorrow for one hour. Tell your parents you'll be late. Busers, be sure someone is free to pick you up."

Munchmore smiled and rubbed his hands together gently, back and forth, back and forth. His smile was absolutely slimy. Like the grinch.

Miss Tuller turned to Munchmore. "I will stay with them after school tomorrow," she said.

"Oh, no, no, no!" Munchmore raised his pudgy hands. "This is my job. I'll be glad to—"

"I will do it," Miss Tuller said softly. She turned away from him, dismissing him just the way she dismisses a kid.

She looked at Mr. Jackson. He was finished with the messy part and was pouring out the disinfectant. It smelled worse than the throwup.

"Boys and girls, get into your jackets," Miss Tuller said. "You may have a short recess until the room is ready again."

Out on the playground, everybody decided it had been worth it. I thought so, too, even though Grandma was going to be plenty upset when I told her I had to stay after. But Munchmore hadn't found out it was Mimi and Libby and me. So Grandma wouldn't either, as long as Munchmore never found out. And

I was still a little scared that he would, even though nobody else seemed worried.

After recess, Miss Gladstone gave us a library period to do more work on our project about the states. She said she wanted us to include a lot of historical facts in our project, so that's why we needed the library resource books. I think she just made that up on the spot. The real reason was that the room still stank, and she didn't want to stay there any more than we did. Of course, it was all Carrie's fault, but she got to go home.

Actually, nobody really minded. Library period is always fun because we get to go without Miss Gladstone, and instead we get Gwendolyn, the library teacher. Gwendolyn has about a thousand rules, but she can never enforce any of them. Nobody pays any attention to her at all, and it makes her really nuts.

For some reason, Gwendolyn insists that we all call her by her first name. At first, we thought it was because her last name is so weird, but then, Gwendolyn isn't such a terrific name, either. It always makes me think of a dragon. Gwendolyn never told us what her last name is, but Mimi found out by going to the office and looking on the teachers' mailboxes. It's Guggle—Gwendolyn Guggle.

One of her rules is that we can only sit four people to a table. Before I came here, that meant Mimi and Libby and Jennifer and Joy had a table. Four perfect. Now with me, there were five, but we always tried to get away with it anyway.

That day, as soon as we sat down in the library with our books, Gwendolyn appeared at the table.

"There are five people at this table," she said.

Nobody looked up. That's one of the things I learned right away, because the person who looks up is the one who gets sent away. That person gets to sit at a separate table with someone like weird Andrew. Or Carrie. And thinking of Carrie made me wonder again if she'd tell Munchmore on us.

"There are five people at this table!" Gwendolyn said again. It was the exact same thing she had said a minute before, only this time she said it louder.

Why do grown-ups always say the obvious?

Still nobody looked up.

She rapped the table with her pencil. Her perfume smells like dead roses, and as she moves, it sort of blows over you, practically choking you.

Libby kept her head bent over her books, but she made a big thing of wrinkling up her nose.

"You!" Gwendolyn tapped Libby on the head with her pencil. "What's your name?"

"It's Libby," Libby said. She rubbed her head. "And that wasn't nice."

"Move!" Gwendolyn said. "Four to a table."

"I was here first," Libby said. She looked down at her books again.

Gwendolyn puffed a little bit, but she didn't say anything more. She just stood there over us.

Finally, Mimi sighed and stood up. "Okay, okay," she said, in this martyr kind of voice. "I'll go."

Gwendolyn looked very relieved, even though she didn't say anything. She just walked away, probably to another table to bother somebody else.

"Come on," Mimi said quietly to me. "Get your

stuff." Libby and Jennifer and Joy were already gathering up their things.

"What's up?" I asked.

"Just come on," Mimi said.

I got my books together and followed Mimi to another table. So did Libby. And Jennifer. And Joy.

All five of us sat down at the next table.

It was really hard not to laugh. But the others just went on reading their books like nothing at all had happened. I wondered when Gwendolyn would notice.

After a few minutes, I got up and got a book on Connecticut, put out by the Historical Society. It told all about historical houses and inns. Just what I needed to know about. And not just for my report. All day I had been thinking about that plan I needed to talk about with Mimi and Libby. I put the book aside to check out when library period was over. Then I found one on battles fought in New York, and so I put that one with the other. I didn't think there'd been any battles fought in Grandpa's house, but it didn't hurt to get the book anyway. When I didn't see Gwendolyn anywhere, I sneaked over to where the fiction books were, and got two of my favorites— *Anne of Green Gables* and *Anne of Avonlea*. Back at the table, I put them in the pile with my other books. I missed having all my favorite books from home with me at Grandma's.

Suddenly, for no reason at all, I felt tears come to my eyes. I missed my books. I missed my mom and dad. I was mad about the baby and scared about the house. Everybody else was having fun playing tricks on teachers, and I felt plain unhappy all of a sudden. I quick bent over the table, pretending I was making a neat pile of my books, just like I had seen Carrie do that first day when I'd come back here. Why was I suddenly so unhappy? I kept my head bent over my books, and blinked about a thousand times to keep the tears back.

It was just time to check out our books and go back to class when Gwendolyn saw that there were five of us at the table. Or when she decided to let us know she'd seen us. She let out a yell that made me drop my whole pile of books.

"If that happens again, you will fail library!" she yelled.

Libby looked at me. "I'm real scared," she said.

"Me, too," Mimi said. "Look at my knees. They're shaking."

I bent down and picked up my books. Mimi and Libby and Jennifer and Joy were already on their way out of the library, all of them laughing together. I hadn't said anything, but I couldn't help feeling a little sorry for Gwendolyn. I mean, she couldn't control anybody. She really shouldn't have been a teacher.

I sighed. It stinks not to be able to control things. It really does.

I brought my books up to the counter to check them out. I felt a little shy, but I tried smiling at Gwendolyn. She looked surprised, but she smiled back. And then I thought: she'd never believe this in a million years ... but I bet I know exactly how she feels.

Mimi, Libby, and I were walking home together that day, when Mimi suddenly poked me and pointed up ahead. "Carrie!" she said.

Carrie was sitting on the green bench by the corner, where Mimi and Libby and I always sit.

"That's *our* bench," Mimi said.

"What's she doing on it?" Libby said.

When we got closer, we saw that Carrie looked just as pale and creepy as she had earlier. Only difference was, she didn't seem quite as puky-looking as she had in the morning.

"You're supposed to be sick," Mimi said to her.

"I was before," she said. "I'm better now."

"You have to stay home—in the house—if you get sent home sick," I told her. "That's the rule."

"I couldn't," she said. "I had to do something."

"What?" Mimi, Libby, and I all said it at the same time.

Carrie got that blank, wide-eyed expression on her face like she does sometimes. Mimi always says it makes her look exactly like a dead fish. "It was wrong what happened this morning," Carrie said.

"Yeah," Mimi said. "It was gross when you puked."

"I didn't mean *that*," Carrie said. She glared at Mimi. "I got sick because I should have told and I didn't. So I have to tell now. It's the *right* thing to do."

We just all stared at her.

"Right?" I said. "But you promised!"

"Sometimes you have to break a promise," she said. She blinked, a long, slow blink, like a fish that was falling asleep. I wondered if fish sleep.

"Tell and we'll get you," Mimi said real quietly.

"I'm not scared," Carrie said. But she began twisting her mittens around in her hands. "My brother said I ought to tell everybody." Her fish eyes looked at me. "Even your grandma. Mimi's a very bad influence on you, my brother said."

"Your brother's an even bigger jerk than you are," Libby said.

"Tell and we'll get you," Mimi said again.

"Will you stop it?" Carrie yelled. She suddenly burst out crying. "Well, if I don't tell, I'll keep on throwing up," she wailed. She wiped her nose on her balled-up mittens. The snot made gray streaks on them. "My brother said so and he knows. He's going to be a psychiatrist when he grows up. He said I was throwing up because I had to get rid of something. And if I don't get rid of it by telling, I'll keep throwing up."

"Hey, that would be cool," Mimi said, looking at Libby and me. "Then we'd get free recess every day." She turned to Carrie, and then she said, real slowly, as though every word was a separate sentence, "Your. Brother. Is. Spooky."

"My brother is smart," Carrie said. "And you're just jealous."

"You tell," Mimi said. "And *all* of us will swear it was your idea."

"So?" Carrie said. "Nobody'd believe you."

"Bet," Libby said.

"Bet," I said. "There's . . . fifteen kids in the class?" I said it as a question, as if I didn't really know, but I knew exactly how many kids there were. "And fourteen of us will swear it was your idea," I said. It seemed kind of mean, but she'd started it.

"Yeah," Mimi said. "We'll even say we tried to talk you out of doing it, but you insisted."

"You wouldn't!" Carrie yelped.

"We would." All three of us said it together.

"But that's not fair!" Carrie sobbed.

"Fair?" I said. "Look who's talking about fair!"

And just like that, Carrie jumped up off the bench and took off running. But not into school—away from it, heading toward home, running like a ghost was after her. I wondered what her brother would tell her this time.

Mimi and Libby started to laugh, but I said, "Suppose her *brother* tells?"

Mimi just shrugged. "We blame it on his sister." She grinned.

I wished I could be as cheerful about it as Mimi was. And when I told Grandma that night that I had to stay after next day, she wasn't cheerful, either. She was absolutely grumpy.

Next day, three things happened: One, Carrie didn't show up in school all day. I wondered if she was home still throwing up. Two, Miss Tuller kept us after school and made us each write a composition on "Changing." Nobody knew what she wanted in it, and she wouldn't tell. She said we had to figure it out ourselves. And three, Carrie's brother came to the classroom door while we were writing, and he asked to talk with Miss Tuller. Miss Tuller said no, go home.

When the hour was up, Miss Tuller collected all of the papers. She said, "Now, boys and girls, I trust that nothing like this will happen again. As far as I'm concerned, this matter is over and done with. I will listen to no more discussion of it. From *anyone*."

As we left, she stood at the door and shook hands with each of us, very formal and serious, the way she did last fall on the first day of school. When it was my turn, my heart was racing. She took my hand and held it just a moment longer than she had anyone else's. "The matter is finished," she said very quietly.

I nodded. I thought I knew what she meant. She

meant that she already knew who had done it, and she wasn't going to say one more word about it—not to Mr. Mountmore, not to Grandma, not to anybody. Not even to me.

It was the first time in my whole, entire life that I've ever felt like hugging a teacher.

12

Next day when Mimi, Libby, and I were walking to school together, I said, "I've been thinking about them maybe tearing down Grandpa's house."

"Yeah?" Mimi said.

"I've been thinking of a plan. But I need some help. Fast." I hesitated, and then I said, "Because they might get a baby, and—"

"What?" Libby practically yelled it. "Your grandmother's going to have a baby?"

"Really?" Mimi said. "You mean she and your grandfather still. . . ?"

"Mimi!" I said.

She grinned.

"Not my grandmother," I said, glaring at her. "Actually . . . my parents. But they're not going to *have* a baby. They're going to . . . adopt one."

"Hey, that's cool!" Mimi said. "We have a baby cousin, Leigh. And she's—"

"A pain," Libby said.

"That's just because she peed in your lap the other day," Mimi said, laughing.

"You wouldn't think it was funny if she did it to you," Libby said, real grumpy like.

Mimi just laughed again, but I could see that made Libby mad.

Mimi turned to me. "A baby! I don't think I'd want a baby around." But then, before I could even agree, she said, "Leigh's cute, though. She's got this stuffed bunny that she drags around by its ears everywhere she goes. Maybe your baby'll be cute, too."

"Leigh's okay," Libby said. "When she doesn't pee on you. So what's a baby got to do with your grandma's house?"

I didn't think I wanted to tell them what I'd been thinking lately—that if I didn't like the baby I might want to live with Grandma and Grandpa. So instead I said, "We got to do something about the house. Fast. And I've got a plan."

"Yeah?" Mimi said. "What?" She stopped dead still in the middle of the sidewalk. All you have to say to Mimi to get her interest is "I got a plan."

"Well," I said. "We know it's an old house, but Grandpa doesn't know if it's historical. But if it is, and we—you and Libby and me—can find out for sure . . ." I looked down at the library books in my arms. "Then it says in here that they can't tear it down. I think. And Grandpa thinks so, too."

"So how do we find out?" Libby said. "Ask somebody?"

"Not *ask*, silly!" Mimi said impatiently. "You gotta find out yourself and then tell them."

"How do you know?" Libby said.

" 'Cause I do. I bet anything that we have to *prove* it's old, like find something old . . ." Mimi turned to me, her eyes wide. "Maybe we could find a secret passage!"

"That's dumb, Mimi," Libby said. "You don't do that. All you have to do is—"

"Will you two listen?" I said. I said it really loud, because when Mimi and Libby get into these stupid arguments about who knows what, they go on forever. Most of the time neither of them knows what they're talking about.

They both shut up.

"I know we can save it if we can prove it's historical," I said. "And I bet anything it *is*. I even—"

"I'll come up with a plan," Mimi said.

"It'll be a stupid one," Libby said.

"Shush up!" I said, glaring at them. I can't ever figure out why they start to fight. Is that what it's like to have a sister?

"We've got to read the books first," I said. "Find out what to look for. And—" I continued, in this very important voice—"I know where to start looking."

Right away they both shut up and looked at me.

I said the rest real slowly. "In . . . the . . . cellar."

Instantly, Mimi said, "You found something?"

"Yeah, what?" Libby asked.

"Nothing. Yet. But there's a dirt floor down there. We could dig in it and—"

"Yeah!" Both twins said it at once. It was the first time they had agreed on anything that day.

"Maybe we'll find Indian artifacts!" Libby said.

Mimi looked like she was going to argue with Libby, but after a second all she said was "When?"

"Saturday. Grandpa's real busy in the store on Saturdays and Grandma helps him. So no one will know what we're doing."

"Yeah." Mimi's eyes were shining.

"Saturday, then?" I said.

"Saturday." They both said it at the same time. Then they looked at each other and they both started to laugh. Mimi tucked her arm in Libby's like they were best friends again.

I didn't think I'd ever understand sisters.

On Saturday when I woke up it was snowing. When Mimi and Libby got there, I put on my boots and coat and mittens as if I were going out with them to play in the snow. Instead, after we went out the kitchen door, we headed for the basement.

The apartment is right over Grandpa's store. When you go out the kitchen door, you're at the top of a flight of steps. You go down them, and at the bottom you're in a little hallway. There are three doors there. One goes into the store. One door goes out to the street. And one leads to the basement storage room.

We looked over our shoulders and up the stairs.

Nobody. We looked through the glass window into the store. Grandpa and Grandma were both busy with customers. I picked up a snow shovel that was standing in the hall. Then, very quietly, we opened the basement door, went in, and pulled the door closed behind us.

"Stink—y!" Libby whispered.

I felt for the light switch and turned it on. Libby was holding her nose.

Mimi ran down the steps in front of us.

I ran down after her, lugging the snow shovel with me. Mimi had said the other day that you shouldn't use shovels for this kind of digging. She said it was an archaeological dig, so we should use spoons. I didn't care what Mimi said. You couldn't dig up anything with a spoon.

Libby stayed at the top of the stairs. "It stinks down here," she complained. "It's almost as bad as Munchmore."

"But not as bad as the sewer," I said. Mimi and Libby and I once took the lid off a manhole and went down in a sewer. That really stank.

"Ooh, yeah," Mimi said. "Remember the rats in the sewer? We should try and catch one and put it in Munchmore's car." She laughed. "Maybe there's rats down here, too."

Libby screamed. "That's not funny," she said.

"Will you shush up?" I said.

"*Are* there rats down here?" she said.

She was still at the top of the stairs. She's scared of a lot of things, but she's really terrified about rats.

I looked at her. I was tempted to say, "Maybe," just to tease her, but knowing her, she'd scream again. So instead I said, "No rats."

"I found my spot to dig!" Mimi called. She had already disappeared to the back part of the basement, where the dirt floor was. I followed her. It was even darker and smellier back there.

"Hey, you guys, wait up," Libby called.

Mimi was kneeling in a dark corner, digging with her spoon. I decided to dig in front of a door on the same wall where she was working. The door used to lead to the outside but now it was all boarded up. I had a special reason for choosing it. I had read in one of the library books that somebody once dug in the cellar of an old schoolhouse and found slate pencils under a door, as if people had dropped them when they were coming in, and the pencils somehow just got buried there. If anything was dropped by this door, I'd find it.

"It's spooky down here," Libby said, when she joined us.

"Ooooh!" Mimi moaned, like she was a ghost.

I put a hand around my throat, stretched out my neck, and made a gurgling sound like I was choking.

"Funny!" Libby said sarcastically. She made a face at both of us.

All of us began digging then, even Libby. Libby was using a little trowel, the kind you use to plant flowers. She was digging very carefully, as if she expected skeletons to jump out of the dirt or something. Mimi was digging furiously with her spoon. Knowing her, she was probably *hoping* to find a skel-

94

eton. I hated to admit it, but she was doing better with the spoon than I was with the shovel. The ground was so hard-packed that it was like concrete, and the shovel only sort of scraped the dirt around a little.

We worked for a very long time, none of us speaking.

"There has to be something here," Mimi said once. She had a small mound of dirt beside her, but that was all.

I nodded, but I didn't answer. There had to be. But I was getting blisters on my hands, and my back and shoulders were hurting.

Libby had stopped digging and was leaning against the wall, picking at the bark that was still on some of the tree trunks that made up the wall.

I looked at my watch. We had worked for one whole hour and hadn't found anything. No slate pencils. Not even an Indian artifact for Libby. Not one single thing.

I began to feel really, really depressed. Time was running out. Grandpa had said it, and he wouldn't say it if it wasn't so. And I couldn't even come up with a discovery to save the house.

"I give up," I said at last. I straightened up. "Let's quit."

Mimi seemed disappointed, but I could tell she agreed with me.

Then I looked at Libby and she had a funny look on her face, wide-eyed like she was scared. "What's that?" she whispered.

"What?" I said.

"That sound. Listen!"

I listened, but I didn't hear anything. I looked at Mimi. She was frowning like she was listening, too. "What is it?" Libby whispered again. She backed away from the wall where she'd been standing.

We were all quiet again, listening, and Mimi made a face. "You're faking," she said. "There's nothing."

"I mean it," Libby said. "There is." She was clutching the front of her jacket to her, and she looked absolutely terrified.

"A rat?" Mimi said, grinning.

But Libby didn't even scream. She just stood there, frozen.

Mimi and I looked at each other. At first I thought Libby was just teasing us, getting back at Mimi and me for teasing her before, but then I heard it, too. It was a low sound—like a sigh, but louder.

Mimi made this weird little scared sound and put her hand up to her throat.

All three of us dropped our things and huddled together. And then we heard it again, right next to us, a big, deep sigh that seemed to come from between the boards in the wall right where we were standing. A person, taking a deep, shivery breath.

"Let's get out of here," I said.

Even Mimi didn't argue. I grabbed the shovel, and Mimi scooped up her spoon. Libby didn't stop to get her trowel. All three of us raced for the stairs.

We were practically pushing one another up the steps. When we were halfway up, I said, "It wasn't anything. Just some air or something. Right?"

Nobody answered.

When we got to the top, we paused. It felt safer up there by the door. "We'll come down later," Mimi said. "Peek between the boards."

"*You* peek between the boards," Libby whispered. "Not me."

"But something's in there," Mimi said.

"Some*body*, you mean," I said.

"A ghost!" Mimi said. "Our troubles would be over! That would *prove* it's historical!"

"You're weird," Libby said.

I didn't say anything. But I secretly agreed with Libby. Mimi was definitely weird if she thought this meant our troubles were over. The baby was coming, the house was going to be torn down, Grandma and Grandpa were going to move away, and I'd never come back or go to school there or see Mimi and Libby again. And Mimi thought our troubles were over!

Unless . . . Mimi couldn't be right, could she? Would having a ghost really make a house historical? I had heard of ghosts in old houses. Would it really make a difference to the people who were going to tear down the house? It might. But . . . I shuddered just thinking about it. Because I didn't care if it was a historical ghost or just a plain one. It meant that I was living in the same house with a ghost. And if I really wanted to save the house—then I might have to do what Mimi said. I might have to go down in the cellar again. And face a ghost.

13

Mimi and Libby and I didn't go down there anymore that day. Mimi said she just didn't feel like it. I had a feeling that she was as scared as Libby and me but wouldn't admit it. Then next day, Sunday, we couldn't because Mimi and Libby were gone all day at a family reunion. I didn't mind. I was very relieved to have a reason to put it off.

Next day when we got into school, Miss Gladstone was busy doing the usual Monday morning money stuff—collecting milk money and selling lunch tickets. Also, our class was getting ready to go to the Museum of Science and Industry, so she had to get that money. While she was collecting it, she said, "Boys and girls, please sit down and use your time wisely."

Right away, Mimi, Libby, and I pulled our desks together. We opened up our social studies books as if we were doing our project on the states. Instead, Mimi had brought in her collection of Garbage Pail Kids cards, and we began spreading them out on the desk behind the books.

While we were doing it, Mimi said, "You know about the ghost in—"

Immediately, Libby started going, "La, la, la, blah, blah, blah." She stuck her fingers in her ears at the same time.

"Let's go down the cellar after school," Mimi said, ignoring her. "Peek through the cracks and see if we can see him."

"You really believe there's a ghost?" I asked, because I wasn't sure I believed it. I mean, half of me thought it was stupid. Half of me was scared, too. But then, what was I scared of if there was no such thing?

"Yeah?" Mimi said. "Don't you? And if we could prove it, then nobody could tear the house down. And wouldn't it be exciting to really *see* it?"

"Yeah, real exciting!" Libby said sarcastically. She had taken her fingers out of her ears and was making a face at Mimi. "While he's stabbing you to death."

"Ghosts don't stab you," Mimi said. "They just suck your breath away."

Libby screamed and stuffed her fingers back in her ears again.

Miss Gladstone looked up, frowning. "Girls!" she said.

We quick bent our heads over our books again. Mimi gave Libby a poke. Libby poked back.

"Boys and girls," Miss Gladstone said after a minute. "Choose partners now and line up for library, please."

Right away, everybody scrambled to pair up. Libby left us and immediately chose Joy. I knew that meant she was still mad at Mimi.

Mimi grabbed me for her partner. "So?" she said quietly. "You gonna do it?"

And have a ghost suck my breath away? No way. "I don't know," I said. I tried to sound casual. "I'll let you know after school."

Then Mimi and I raced to the front of the room so we could be first in line. We got there just in front of Michael and Jay. I really couldn't wait to get to the library. I was going to ask Gwendolyn for help—not that I'd tell her exactly what I was looking for, or tell her anything at all about ghosts. But maybe she could help me find books that would show how to tell if a house was historical. I could find the rest, the ghost part, by myself.

While we waited for the rest of the class to line up, Mimi and I looked out in the hall. We saw Munchmore waddling down the hall toward the cafeteria. During his free periods, he always sits at a table in the cafeteria even when it's not lunchtime, as if he's just waiting and thinking about food. Once, Mimi hid under one of the tables for an entire period to watch him, but the only interesting thing he did was blow his nose into notebook paper.

While everybody was grabbing partners and lining up, Carrie walked right by Mimi and me, pretending like she hadn't seen us. She hadn't spoken to either of us since the day she'd said she was going to tell about the sweater.

"You know what?" Mimi said quietly to me. "We never got even with her. Let's bombard her with spitballs in the library when Gwendolyn's not looking. Pass it on."

She turned around and whispered it to Michael.

I turned around and told Jay.

"Pass it on," we both said.

In a minute, everybody was in line, and everybody had gotten the message. We all filed out of the classroom, Mimi and I leading. I looked around then and saw that everybody was lined up in twos with a friend. Except for Carrie. She had Miss Gladstone as her partner. I couldn't help feeling sorry for her again, at least a little bit. I mean, she is a jerk. But I'd just hate to be left out the way she is.

When we got to the library, right away I left Mimi and went to the place where the history books are kept. They're in a corner, behind a big book stack, sort of off by themselves. I picked one and looked through it. It told lots about historical houses, but hardly anything at all about how to tell what made a house historical. It seemed like all the historical houses had already been discovered. There were a lot of other books, so I sat down on the floor and pulled out some more. I must have had about twenty books spread out around me, when I looked up and saw Gwendolyn standing over me. Uh-oh.

"I'm going to put them back," I said quickly.

"That's all right," she said. She didn't seem mad. "I like to see people interested in books."

"You do?" I said.

"I *am* a librarian, you know," she said.

"Oh." I was a little embarrassed. I did know that, but it surprised me that she liked to see people using her books. I guess I always thought that it annoyed her to have people in the library—that she'd rather have her books to herself.

"Something I can help you find?" she asked.

I hesitated. I couldn't really say, "Yes, tell me if having a ghost in a house means people can't tear the house down." But maybe I could just sort of hint. So I said, "I'm trying to find out—well, what do you need in a house to make it historical? I mean, how do you find out if it is or not?"

"Usually there's a plate on the front of the house that tells you," she said. "Or you could call the Brooklyn Historical Society and they could—"

"No," I said. "That's not what I meant. I meant, suppose nobody knew that it was—yet. Like, how could you prove it?"

"Well," Gwendolyn said. "That's a hard one. But you could research it—look up what makes a historical landmark, what kind of things to look for."

She reached for one of the books I had there. "I remember reading in one of these books about mantels. . . ." She flipped through the book slowly. "Somewhere it said that if you find an oversized mantel, that could mean that the fireplace was once much bigger than it is now. Or, if you get down and look up inside the chimney—" She broke off and smiled at me. "Children would love that, wouldn't they?" she said. "Crawling around inside fireplaces."

I nodded and smiled back at her.

She went on then about other stuff, but none of it had anything to do with Grandpa's house.

She must have noticed that I wasn't too interested, because she stopped in mid-sentence. She frowned at her skirt and dusted something off it. "Well," she said, "does that help at all?"

I started to say no. But then I thought—she was trying to be helpful. And she did seem to know about research, anyway. So even though it sounded stupid, I decided to try it.

I brushed at my skirt, too. "Would having a ghost in the cellar of an old house make the house historical?" I asked.

I expected her to laugh. I really did.

"I don't know about a ghost," she said slowly. She sounded serious, not at all as if she were laughing at me. "I've never heard that proven, though people are always saying there's a ghost in this house or that. But cellars *are* sometimes the best place to look for things in old houses. I just saw that in that book I was looking through a minute ago."

"Yeah," I said. I sighed. We'd already done that.

"And some of the best things are right in plain sight," she said.

"Like what?" I asked.

"The floor," she said, smiling. "The walls themselves. Some walls are made right out of tree trunks, with the bark still on them. Now those, I bet, are the really old ones."

"*What?*" I said. "*Tree* trunks?"

And then I ducked, because spitballs were flying everywhere. They flew over the shelves and landed all around us, like we were in the middle of a snowstorm.

Gwendolyn looked around, startled.

From somewhere on the other side of the library, I heard Carrie screech.

Gwendolyn jumped up. She knocked over her chair as she started around to the other side of the stacks.

"Can't I leave you people alone for one single minute?" she yelled.

"Wait!" I called after her. I wanted to say, "What did you say about the walls? About tree trunks? Like in Grandpa's cellar?" But she was already gone.

I followed her around the other side. There was a mess of spitballs—tables, floors, bookshelves—spitballs flying everywhere. The minute Gwendolyn and I appeared, it all stopped as if by magic. All the kids were studying and reading their books and looking perfectly innocent. All but Carrie. She was standing up by a table, brushing soggy little paper balls off her and out of her hair and yelling at the top of her lungs. "I saw them, Gwendolyn!" she said. "Mimi and Michael started it, Gwendolyn. I saw them."

I decided I didn't feel at all sorry for her anymore.

14

When Miss Gladstone heard about what happened in the library, she said we couldn't have lunch recess that day, that we had to stay in the cafeteria all lunchtime and read. Everybody was real grumpy about it, but I didn't care that much. It was cold out that day anyway. Besides, I had my book, *Anne of Green Gables*, with me to read. It was my favorite book, even though I had already read it seven times.

At lunchtime, the minute I told Mimi and Libby what Gwendolyn had said about the cellar, Mimi insisted we call the Brooklyn historical place. Right away. "Now!" she said.

"Can't," I said. "There's no phone booth in this school. You know that."

"I know," Mimi said. She looked across the cafeteria to where the teachers were sitting having lunch. "But Miss Tuller's over there."

"So?" I said.

"So, let's sneak in her office and use her phone."

"No way!" I said.

"Why not?"

I hesitated.

"She won't know," Mimi said.

I still hesitated. We were in enough trouble for now. What if we got caught? But I really didn't want to wait till after school, either.

"I'm not doing it," Libby said.

Mimi just ignored her. "C'mon, Jeremy," she said to me. "Who's going to know? And we got to find out about the house!"

"Okay," I said. "If you promise to be the lookout."

"You're gonna get caught, and you're gonna be in trouble, and you're gonna be sorry," Libby said.

Mimi just made a face at Libby.

Mimi and I raced through the rest of our lunch. We decided we'd tell Miss Steinborn, the lunch monitor, that we had to go to the lavatory. It was the only way we'd be able to get into the hall—and from there to the office—since after lunch we were being punished. We didn't even finish half our lunch. Not that it mattered that much. Hot lunch that day was turkey cubes on rice with peas. At least, that's what the lunch lady called it. It was really turkey fat. And the peas were the super-big mushy kind.

The whole time we were eating, Libby didn't speak to us.

But then, when Mimi and I got up to go, Libby stood up, too. All three of us went and returned our trays, put our silverware in the bowls, and then dumped our lunches in the trash. We put the empty plates at the plate window and went to the cafeteria door.

Miss Steinborn was standing guard there, her arms folded over her huge chest. "Go back and sit down," she said. "You're being punished."

"I know," I said. "But I have to go. Bad."

"You're supposed to do that before lunch," she said.

"I did," I said. "But I have to do it again."

"It's the hot lunch," Mimi said, real seriously. "It makes you go. Even if you're being punished."

Miss Steinborn heaved her chest a couple of times, but finally she said, "All right." She glared at us. "But you be back in this room in five minutes or I'm coming in after you."

"Yes, Miss Steinborn." We said it as politely as if we were talking to Miss Tuller. And then we were out in the hall. Free.

It was silent out there, nobody around. Our school is so small that everybody has lunch at the same time. The only sounds were the hum of some computers from the Career Center across the hall, and the gurgling of a fish tank in a classroom somewhere.

"Five minutes," Mimi whispered, looking at her watch. "It's twelve-twenty."

"We're going to get caught," Libby whispered. "You wait and see. And then—"

"Let's go," I said, not wanting to hear what Libby thought would happen to us.

All three of us raced on tiptoe down the hall to Miss Tuller's office. Libby kept stopping to look over her shoulder. The door to the office was closed. All of us took a last look around, then sneaked inside and closed the door after us.

I went over to the desk, picked up the phone, and dialed Information. My heart was just racing. When the information person answered, I said quietly, "Brooklyn Historical Commission, please."

"Information!" the voice said again.

I said it again.

"You'll have to speak up," the voice said.

Speak up? I already felt as if I were shouting. But I said it again, just a little louder. "Brooklyn Historical Commission, please!" I said.

"One moment, please."

While I waited, Mimi shoved a pad of Miss Tuller's paper across the desk for me to write on. The desk was completely neat—only a desk blotter, some pads of paper, and a pen in a shiny penholder. Mimi took the pen out of the penholder and handed that to me, too. I wondered if fingerprints really did show up on stuff.

After a second, the information person came back. "I'm sorry," she said. "There is no Brooklyn Historical Commission."

"What?" I said it too loud. Then, in practically a whisper, I added, "But there must be."

"There is a Brooklyn Historical *Society*," the voice said, real snooty like.

"All right," I said. "Give me that."

"I don't like it in here," Libby whispered.

I wrote down the number, hung up on Information, and dialed the other number as fast as I could. Miss Tuller has one of the old kinds of phone dials—the kind that goes around in circles, not the push-button kind. It takes much longer to dial, and I was getting really scared.

"One minute, fifteen seconds gone," Mimi said, looking at her watch.

Somebody was speaking in my ear: "Historical Society." And I didn't know what to say!

"Uh . . ." I turned to the twins. "What?" I said.

"How do you find out if a house is historical?" Libby prompted in a whisper.

"No," Mimi said. "Do tree trunks in the basement—"

"I'm trying to find out something," I said into the phone, trying to talk quietly and still be heard at the same time. "See, there's this house . . . it's my grandfather's. I want to find out if it's historical or not."

"I'll give you our library," the voice said.

I rolled my eyes.

"What?" Libby whispered.

"They're giving me the library."

"Two minutes," Mimi said.

When the next voice answered, I went through the whole thing again and then found out: I was still talking to the wrong place! I had to call something called the Landmarks Preservation Committee. The person gave me the number and I wrote that down.

"Three minutes," Mimi said.

Libby looked like she was getting ready to have a nervous breakdown.

But I was just getting mad. This was stupid. I quick dialed the number I had gotten and when somebody answered, I went through the whole thing again. *Twice.* First I told the woman who answered the phone, and then I had to tell it all over again to a man in the Research Department—a man with the weirdest voice I'd ever heard—loud but fuzzy, too, with the words sort of blurring together. In my head, I immediately named him The Voice. When I was all finished telling for the fourth time, and after I gave my name and address, all The Voice promised to do was send me a form to fill out.

"A *form?*" I said. "I don't know how to fill out a form." I felt suddenly as if I was going to cry. "Besides," I said. "There's no time for forms."

"Four minutes, ten seconds," Mimi said, like she was counting down to an execution.

"Is the building threatened with demolition?" The Voice asked.

"With what?"

"Demolition."

"Is that the same thing as being torn down?" I said.

"Same thing."

"Then, yes," I said.

The Voice laughed, but then it said, sort of kindly, "The form isn't hard to fill out. All it asks is name, address of building, what the building is currently used for. A photo, if possible—"

"Okay. Thanks," I said. "Good-bye."

"Wait!" It cleared its throat. "There's a space on the form where it asks if the building is threatened with demolition. Answer 'yes' to that. All right?"

"And then what?" I said.

"Five minutes," Mimi said.

"We're going to die," Libby moaned.

"Someone will probably come out and look at it. And then . . . well, there are a lot of things we might do. But that's a first step."

"Will it take long?" I asked.

"It's taking *forever!*" Libby whispered, glaring at me. She kept looking toward the door and jiggling around like she was nervous. Or maybe she really did have to go to the bathroom.

There was a pause on the other end of the phone, and then The Voice said, "I think if this house is worth seeing . . . and if it's threatened with demo . . . with being torn down . . . then, no, it won't take long. We could have someone out there in . . . maybe a week."

"You promise?" I said.

"Promise. Send it to my attention—Pat Calvert— and I'll take care of it myself."

"Thank you," I said. I started to say good-bye, but before I could, Mimi had grabbed the phone from me and hung it up.

"She's coming!" she whispered.

I turned to the door. Through the glass in the door window, we could see Miss Tuller coming down the hall. She had her head bent, reading a piece of mail or something in her hand.

I looked around frantically. What could we do? There was only one door. If we went out, she'd have to see us!

Then I saw it—the closet door! Without stopping to think, I grabbed Mimi's and Libby's arms and pulled them toward the closet. Libby must not have had time to think either, or she'd have started to yell. I yanked the door open. And then all three of us were shoving and tumbling our way inside.

15

We stood, huddling together, jammed back against the coats. We hadn't slammed the door shut tight behind us. It stood open just a crack, so we could see directly out at Miss Tuller's desk, but we couldn't see the door to the hall.

We knew when she came in the room, though, because there was a click and the lights went on. But she didn't come to her desk. Where was she? Was she just standing by the door looking around? Did she know we were there? Why did I *do* this?

For what seemed like three weeks, nothing happened. I could hear my heart beating so loudly I was sure Mimi and Libby could hear it and maybe Miss Tuller could, too. Suddenly we saw her, crossing the room to her desk. She stopped, frowning.

Oh, no! We had left the telephone numbers and her pen and the papers all over the desk!

I know I stopped breathing.

She picked up the papers and frowned at them. Then she looked up and around the room as if she expected to see someone there.

I closed my eyes.

Opened them again.

She frowned down at the papers again. Then, while we watched, she picked up the phone. Slowly, reading from the paper, she dialed one of the numbers. We could see her listening, and then she said, in that formal and polite voice she has, "I'm so very sorry. I must have dialed the wrong number." And she just hung up, very softly.

She kept standing there with that paper in her hand as if she was a statue or something. Oh, no, how long was she going to stay in the room? All afternoon? It was completely hot and stifling in the closet. We'd die of suffocation in here, and nobody'd even know it.

After a minute, Miss Tuller moved and very slowly and carefully began straightening up the desk. First she put the pen back in the penholder. Then she put the pads right in the center of the blotter. And then she put the papers with the phone numbers into the pocket of the black suit she always wears. She walked across the room and disappeared from our sight.

Two things happened next. They happened at exactly the same time: There was a click as the lights went out. And Mimi got the hiccups. The loud, ridiculous hiccups she gets sometimes like nobody else gets. She clamped a hand over her mouth, her eyes wide. But it was too late. If Miss Tuller was still in the room, she'd heard it.

We waited. And waited.

Nothing.

Was Miss Tuller there? Had she heard the hiccups and was waiting?

Mimi hiccuped again. And again. Libby began to make a small gasping sound, like she was crying. Mimi had both hands over her mouth, trying to be quiet, so the hiccups she was making now didn't come out quite as loud as that first one. But you could still hear them.

We waited some more. There was no sound in the room. Not one single sound. Just Mimi hiccuping and Libby gasping like that.

I felt as though I waited three more weeks before I finally got the courage to start inching the closet door open. I knew I'd have to do it myself. Libby wouldn't 'cause she's such a scaredy-cat she'd have stayed in there till June. Mimi couldn't because she had both hands over her mouth.

Slowly I opened the door, inch by inch. My heart was beating wildly. Yet I hardly even cared anymore. It would almost have been a relief to see Miss Tuller there, just to get it over with.

But she wasn't there. When I got the door open and we peeked around it, no one was there. The room was absolutely empty. The desk was clean and neat, like nobody had ever been there.

Super-quietly, on tiptoe, we went to the door and looked through the glass window. No one around.

We opened the door. No one in the hall.

And then we got out of there.

Like maniacs, we ran down the hall to the lavatory and pushed open the swinging door. Safe. Inside. Safe! I didn't care if Steinborn came in now. I didn't care if she screamed and yelled and went on like a cuckoo bird. I didn't care about anything. We were safe!

Mimi hiccuped, a massive, giant-sized hiccup.

Libby was still gasping and making little mewing sounds like a cat crying. But when I looked at her, she wasn't crying. She wasn't crying at all. She was leaning against the edge of the sink, laughing so hard that she could hardly stand up.

Laughing? Libby, the scaredy cat? I just stared at her.

Mimi made a face at her. "It wasn't . . . *hic!* . . . funny, Lib!"

"It was!" Libby gasped. "Ohmigod! It was. It was the funniest thing that ever happened. That hiccup!"

Suddenly, watching Libby, I couldn't help it. I started to laugh, too.

Mimi just glared at us. But then she started to smile, and then she started to laugh. And then she was hiccuping. And laughing. And hiccuping. And laughing.

The door flew open, and Steinborn stood in the doorway. "I've been watching for you!" she shouted. "I've been watching. I told you to be back in the cafeteria in five minutes or I'd come in after you. What are you up to? Get out!"

All three of us were hysterical laughing by then. And Mimi's hiccups were incredible.

"Out!" Steinborn said.

Mimi and I started to leave.

"I can't!" Libby gasped. "I can't."

"Why?" Steinborn said.

"I'm going to wet my pants," Libby said. She fled into one of the stalls and we heard her lock the door.

"One of these days you're going to go just too far," Steinborn said, glaring at Mimi. "And you," she said, looking at me. "You used to behave. What's gotten into you?"

Just then, as we went out in the hall, we saw Miss Tuller standing by the cafeteria door. She watched us come out of the lavatory.

She didn't say one word, but she nodded at us.

We said, "Good afternoon, Miss Tuller," like we had been taught to do.

Seeing her there, I was suddenly scared again, but still I couldn't stop laughing, although not quite as hard as before. But Mimi kept laughing—and hiccuping—just as hard as ever. And behind us in the lavatory, I could still hear Libby laughing.

16

For the next week, Mimi, Libby, and I were super-good. We were quiet in class. Had our assignments done on time. Didn't run in the halls, always walked. Didn't stamp up and down the steps. We didn't even bother Carrie. We were so good that even Munch-more noticed. He told Miss Gladstone after music one day that "certain elements" in the class had seemed to reform. Everybody knew who he was talking about. Me and Mimi and Libby. But mostly Mimi. She made a face at him when he turned his back to us.

Whenever we met Miss Tuller in the hall, we were very polite to her, and she was polite back. Every once in a while, she gave us one of those long, silent looks like she can do. That made me worry a little, because it was as if she knew. Just like I figured she knew about the sweater. But with her, it's always as if—even if she knows you did something you shouldn't—she gives you a chance to make it better. And just in case she knew, Mimi and Libby and I were being super-good.

I was worried about other things, too—like what to tell Grandma and Grandpa about the letter from the Historical Society. And whether or not to tell them that someone might be coming out to look at the house. Mimi, Libby, and I came up wih a plan for both those things, though: I'd tell Grandma and Grandpa that I was getting a letter because of my project on the states. And I wouldn't tell them anything at all about someone coming to see the house.

It would be safer just to let the person show up and tell us that the house was—or wasn't—historical. Whenever I thought about the "wasn't" part, I got *really* worried.

That week was the longest week in my life. Each day seemed like it would never be finished. First I waited for the letter from the Historical Society. After the letter came and Mimi and Libby and I filled out the form, then I waited some more. For Mr. Calvert to come out and see the house.

But he didn't come.

The other thing I waited for was to hear about Stupid Baby. Mom and Dad hadn't called or written in over a week, and I wanted to know what was happening. Actually, only a part of me wanted to know. Another part of me was glad I didn't hear from them. Because if I didn't hear, that meant they weren't coming home with Stupid Baby. Yet.

The one good part about the whole thing was that Mimi didn't try to drag me down into the cellar to see the ghost anymore. Maybe she'd had enough of hiding in dark places after the closet. Or maybe she didn't need to believe in a ghost now that we had something more normal and regular like tree trunks in the cellar.

It was a Sunday evening, almost two whole weeks after the thing in school with Miss Tuller's closet and all, that the phone rang while Grandma and Grandpa and I were finishing supper. I don't know how I knew it was Mom, but I did. I just instantly knew it. I wanted to talk to her! But she was calling to talk about S.B., wasn't she?

When Grandma picked up the phone and began smiling, I knew I'd been right. Mom.

Please, God, I thought, please make something be wrong with the baby. I mean, I don't want it to die or anything like that. But a little thing wrong with it so it has to stay there. Then Mom and Dad will come home, and everything will be just the way it used to be.

Grandma was beckoning to me. "Jeremy?" She was smiling.

Slowly I got up and took the phone from her. "Hello?" I said.

"Honey!" Mom's voice was so clear that it was hard for me to believe that she was in another country. "How are you?"

"Fine," I said, and I suddenly felt shy.

"Oh, Jeremy!" Mom said. "I have so much to tell you. The baby is coming along just—"

"When are you coming home?" I said.

"We're not sure yet. Soon. Three weeks? Maybe four? As soon as Nichole's well enough."

I didn't say anything.

"Is everything all right, Jeremy?"

"Yes." I swallowed hard. "Everything's okay," I said.

Mom laughed, that sweet, deep laugh she has that usually makes me feel that everything's all right. Except it didn't this time. "You don't like to talk on the phone, do you?" Mom said. "That's okay. Would you like to hear about Nichole?"

"Sure," I said. One of the biggest lies I'd told in my whole, entire life.

"All right," Mom said. "She's just three months old, and she's very tiny—no bigger than a newborn, because she's been sick. But since we've been here, she's getting better. And you know why, Jeremy?"

"Why?"

"We think one of the reasons is because every day I go to the hospital and I hold her for a long time. Isn't that amazing? That just holding someone would make a difference like that?"

"Yeah," I said. But you haven't held *me* in a long time. I didn't say it out loud. Besides, that was stupid. I wasn't a baby.

"Jeremy," Mom said. "What is it? Is bringing home a new baby that hard for you?"

"No! It's nothing. I told you, nothing!" I paused,

and then I said, "So are you definitely getting her?"

For a minute, Mom didn't answer. Then she said, "Yes, we are. Jeremy? What? What is it?"

"Nothing. Just wondering."

I heard Mom sigh. "We'll be home in a few weeks," she said softly. "You'll love Nichole, Jeremy. It will take some getting used to, I know. But give it a chance."

"Do I have a choice?" I asked. And instantly felt bad.

But Mom didn't sound upset. She said, "You just have to remember that you'll always be my special girl. Really."

Which probably meant that she wasn't so sure that I would be.

When I didn't say anything, she added, "And I love you so much. Now, would you like to talk to your dad? He's right here and he can't wait to talk with you."

"Okay," I said. And then I said, "I love you, too." Because I do.

Dad came on the phone, and we talked for a minute, and then he asked, "Is everything all right, toots?"

"Fine!" I said. "Why does everybody keep asking that?"

He laughed, but he sounded worried. "Is there anything we can do for you?" he said.

I thought about all the things that would make me happy—to have Grandpa's house be safe. For me to feel good again, not to have to worry anymore. For them to leave the baby there. I couldn't ask for those things. They couldn't give them anyway. So I just said, "There's nothing. I'm fine." And then, because I didn't want him to feel worried, I said, "I'm having fun with the twins. It'll be great if they visit this summer." I tried to sound really cheerful.

"Good," Daddy said. He sounded a little happier. "Okay, toots. We can't wait to be with you again."

After I hung up, I went to my room, closed my door, and got a piece of paper out of my desk. I made a list: Things I Hate About Stupid Baby. It was a long list so it took a long time. It started with ugly, and then it said mean and selfish and a bragger and a double-crosser and a big shot and a pain in the neck and a snob and a tattletale. I realized I wasn't writing about Stupid Baby. I was writing about Carrie. Or maybe Munchmore. But I bet Stupid Baby was a lot like Carrie and like Munchmore, too. And I knew this for sure: The baby took all Mom's attention and time and that's all that Mom talked about or cared about anymore. So selfish was right, anyway. And I bet Mom was holding her right this very second.

I stuck the list in my desk, then picked up Shakesbear and carried him to the window. Everything was going wrong, and I couldn't do anything to stop it. Stupid house. Stupid baby.

I stood at the window looking out at the night. It was clear outside—it had snowed earlier, but now the snow had stopped and the moon was shining on it, and it was all glisteny. I was glad it wasn't dark and spooky-looking out, because ever since we'd been down in the cellar, I'd been scared thinking about a ghost maybe living there. Still, even though it was a pretty night and the moon was shining and making the snow all silvery, it didn't make me feel a whole lot better. And holding Shakesbear didn't make me feel better, either. Because I'd probably have to lock my door to keep Stupid Baby away from my stuffed animals. I held Shakesbear tighter. I wouldn't ever let her touch Shakesbear. Not ever! I went back to my desk and made a big sign to put on my bedroom door—in case I ever went back home. It said: KEEP OUT.

17

There was a knock on my door. I didn't want to talk to anyone, so I didn't say, "Come in." I just said, "What?" I didn't care if I sounded mean.

"Could I talk to you?" It was Grandpa.

"I guess," I said.

Grandpa opened the door and put his head in. "How about some ice cream?" he said.

I shrugged.

"Jensen's is still open," he said.

"Okay!" I said. I threw Shakesbear onto the bed and started to grab my coat and stuff. I love Jensen's. It's this huge ice cream place with big shiny mirrors and revolving lights, and tables that look like they came out of a movie. Grandpa's been taking me there on special occasions ever since I was a little girl. Just him and me together. Never anybody else.

"I'll be waiting," Grandpa said.

It only took me a minute to get ready, and then I went out in the kitchen. Grandma was there, and she insisted that I wouldn't be warm enough—she always says that!—so she made me put on a scarf. She wrapped it around my neck and face until I was practically smothered. All the time she was doing it, she was muttering about how late it was, and I knew she thought I shouldn't be going out. But I've learned from Grandpa what to do when Grandma's like that. He just sort of nods and makes these little sounds, like "Hmm," so she thinks he's listening and agreeing. But then he does exactly what he wants to do anyway. So I did the same thing. But after she finished wrapping me up in the scarf, I gave her a big hug and a kiss good-bye. She hugged me back and smiled at me, so I knew she felt better.

Outside, Grandpa and I walked between the snowbanks, with the moon shining down on us. Above us, the sky was clear, with just small baby clouds scooting along and then passing across the face of the moon. It was like walking in a fairy tale. As usual, neither Grandpa nor I said much, but it felt comfortable. It was nice to be alone with him again. It had been a long time since we'd had time alone. If only Mimi and Libby and I could come up with some way to save the house so Grandpa could stay here and we could always take walks like this! I wondered if we could prove that there was a ghost, if that would make a difference.

After a few blocks, Grandpa said softly, "It doesn't seem fair, does it—the way things happen."

"Nope," I said, sort of automatically. Then I wondered which unfair thing he was talking about. Did he mean me and Mom and Stupid Baby? Or was he talking about himself and the house? But they were both the same, I guess.

"Want to talk about it?" he asked.

"What's to talk about?" I said. "It just stinks."

He nodded.

"You think so, too?" I said.

"Everyone feels that way sometimes," he said.

"You, too?" I insisted.

He put a hand on my shoulder and rested it there for just a minute before taking it away again. "Me, too."

"Really?" I looked up at him. I had been afraid to talk about this because I thought he'd think I was really stupid or selfish or something. "You think it stinks that they're getting a baby?"

He smiled, but he didn't answer directly. Instead he said, "I think that you . . . I . . . have so little control over what's happening right now. And that's hard. That's very hard."

He hadn't said what I had wanted him to say. Still, I felt relieved. He understood. He understood that it stinks not to have control over things. Or people. And for just a minute, I thought of Gwendolyn again and how she couldn't control the class. I reached out and took Grandpa's hand, and he squeezed mine.

We walked hand in hand till we were almost at Jensen's and then I carefully pulled my hand away.

I didn't want to hurt his feelings, but I didn't want to walk in there holding hands, either.

"I love this place!" I said, when we were inside waiting for a table. There were mirrors everywhere, and chandeliers, and overhead fans, and jukeboxes, just like in the olden days. The waitress came and led us to a little round table with a marble top. She gave us menus, but I didn't need one. I knew just what I wanted to have: Fudge Ripple-Marshmallow-M&M-Surprise. It's almost as big as I am.

After she left, I said to Grandpa, "Isn't this place neat?"

Grandpa nodded. "And if it hadn't been for you," he said, "I'd never have come in here."

"Really?"

"Really."

"Then you're lucky you have me."

"I am." He laughed. "But you know what?"

"What?"

"Before you were born, I felt a little bit the way you do now. Not quite sure."

"Not quite sure about what?" I asked.

"Well . . . your dad was the only child I'd ever had." He looked at me as if I should understand something. But I didn't.

"So?" I said.

"So," he said. "I was worried. I didn't know if I could love more than one child."

"Really? But that's so silly!"

He just smiled at me.

"Oh," I said. But I wasn't quite sure I understood.

I mean, maybe I understood. So of course he loved me, too. But it wasn't the same thing at all.

"Well, why do they need another baby?" I said. "You and Grandma only had one."

He just smiled at me.

The waitress came with our ice cream then, and we ate without talking for a while. But all the while, I was thinking: What was Grandpa really saying— that *I* could love a baby, too? Just like he learned to love me? But I couldn't. I knew I couldn't. Or was he trying to tell me that Mom could love another kid besides me? But what about him—Grandpa? Suppose he loved the baby more than me? *Stupid* Baby?

I looked up.

Grandpa was watching me. "I could never love anybody quite the same way that I love you," he said quietly. Like a mind reader.

I was surprised. He'd never told me before that he loved me. I mean, I knew he did. But he'd never said so. Not like Mom who says I love you all the time.

"But you could . . . maybe . . . love . . ." I couldn't say her name. "That baby?" I said.

He nodded.

I went back to eating my ice cream. I didn't know whether I felt bad about his answer or not.

"Okay," I said after a minute. "But you better not ever bring her here."

Grandpa nodded.

"I mean it," I said.

"I understand," Grandpa said.

"You do?"

"Of course." Grandpa looked very serious. "It's our special place."

"Then you won't bring her here?"

"I won't bring her here."

"Promise?"

"Promise."

I took a deep breath and smiled. "Good," I said. And then I said it again. "Good!" Because even though it was silly, probably even selfish, I felt very, very relieved.

We finished our ice cream and walked home together. And we walked hand in hand, just like before.

18

It was an afternoon about two weeks later that I came home from school—and knew right away that something was different.

There were a bunch of cars on the street in front of Grandpa's store. One of them looked like Mom and Dad's car. I knew it couldn't be, though, since they hadn't called to tell me they were coming. But it made me wonder again when they'd be back. Yet with all the cars out there, still there were no customers in the store. And no Grandpa.

"Grandpa?" I called.

No answer.

"Grandpa?"

I looked around. Where was he? Upstairs? But he

never leaves the store alone unless he locks it up.

"Grandpa!"

Then I heard voices. Below me. Downstairs. In the cellar. *The* Voice?

I ran out into the little hallway and opened the cellar door.

There were lights on down there, and the sound of voices.

"Grandpa?" I called.

The murmur of voices stopped. Grandpa called back, "Jeremy? Why don't you come down here?"

I started down the steps. It was Mr. Calvert from the Historical Society down there with Grandpa, wasn't it? It had to be!

I raced down the steps, but suddenly, halfway down, I stopped. This was the first time I'd been down in the cellar since we heard that sound, that ghost sound. But more than that, if this was the person from the Historical Society, that meant that this was my last chance. And suppose Mr. Calvert or whoever said it wasn't a historical house at all?

Then maybe I could tell him about the ghost.

More slowly, I went down the rest of the steps. I followed their voices to the back part of the cellar.

When I got there, I saw that it was all lit up. Big flashlights were on the floor, shining up at the walls. And there wasn't just one man there with Grandpa. There were three men. All of them turned and looked at me when I came in.

Grandpa came and stood beside me. "This is my granddaughter, Jeremy," he said, in that quiet, sort of formal voice he always uses with strangers. "And Jeremy, this is Mr. Schulz. Mr. Freedman." Grandpa waved his hand toward each as he spoke. "And Mr. Calvert."

Mr. Calvert? I stared at them. Mr. Schulz was fat. Mr. Freedman was sneaky-looking. And Mr. Calvert didn't have any hair.

"And you're the young lady who called me," Mr. Calvert said.

It *was* him—The Voice! I'd recognize it anywhere. My heart was racing wildly.

"Yes," I said. My voice came out too small.

"Very smart of you to spot this house as being special," Mr. Calvert said. "Not only is it old, but it has some unique features."

"Does that mean . . . that nobody can tear it down?" I said. I felt as if I'd been waiting to ask that question for a very long time.

Schulz and the other guy laughed. I hate it when grown-ups do that—laugh when you haven't said anything funny. But Mr. Calvert didn't laugh. Neither did Grandpa.

I took a step closer to Grandpa, and he put a hand on my shoulder.

Mr. Calvert said, "We won't know that for a while yet. But if it's as old as we think it is. . . . Maybe."

"First things first," the fat one said.

"A public meeting, I think," the sneaky-looking one said. He had a clipboard and began writing stuff down. "Everybody needs a chance to have their say."

The fat guy was running his fat hand along the

wall beams. "I'm surprised you didn't hear lots of moans and sighs from this cellar," he said. "This kind of construction lets wind whistle right through. People even say it sounds like ghosts."

"Then you mean it *wasn't* a ghost?" I asked. I didn't even mean to say that. It just came out.

The same two guys laughed.

"Well," Grandpa said. "If you gentlemen are finished, I think it's time to get back to work."

Everybody looked at him when he said that, including me. He had a kind of friendly, pleasant look on his face, but I could tell he was waiting for them to move. The fat one and the sneaky one shrugged. Mr. Calvert went over and picked up the flashlights. Then we all went upstairs together.

In the little hallway, everybody shook hands with everybody else. Schulz, the fat one, said they'd be in touch, and then he and Freedman tried to go out the door at the same time. Talk about being in touch! They bumped into each other and I thought for a minute they'd get stuck in the doorway. But they didn't. They only glared at each other, and then they were gone.

After they had left, Mr. Calvert stood for a moment looking at me. And then he said, "You realize you may have found something very important?"

I wanted to ask the question straight out again— and now that the men who had laughed at me were gone, I could. So I said, "They won't tear down the house then?"

"No promises," Mr. Calvert said. "But you've got

a good fighting chance now. And at the very least, there'll be delays while we look into it. You should be very proud of yourself."

I wanted to take the credit for it, but I couldn't. At least, I couldn't take all the credit for the idea. "My librarian helped me," I said truthfully.

He turned to Grandpa then. "If this is as important as I think it is, are you willing to work with us to try and preserve it?"

I looked at Grandpa. Of course! I thought. But Grandpa seemed to be thinking about it. It took him so long to answer that I said, "Grandpa?"

He nodded. "Yes," he said. "Of course." He turned to me then, as though he were talking not to Mr. Calvert, but to me. "It's just hard to realize," he said quietly. "I've been adjusting to losing this place for so long. And now it's all changed."

And *I* changed it, I thought! This house. This store. This place. Safe. All of it saved. And *I* did it!

Mr. Calvert just smiled.

He and Grandpa shook hands, and Mr. Calvert left.

As soon as he was gone, Grandpa and I went in the store. Grandpa went over to the counter and picked up his pipe. He spent a long time lighting it and then puffing on it quietly. He always does that after he's been talking a lot, as if he needs a chance to be quiet with himself.

But I was so excited I could hardly stand it. Very slowly, inside me, this feeling had started to build ever since I first thought it—I did it, I did it! A happy feeling. I could feel it everywhere, from my toes up. I did have a place here. Maybe for good! And I knew I had to call Mimi and Libby right away.

"I've got to call Mimi and Libby," I said. I went to the phone that was on the counter. I called the twins and told them to come over in a hurry. I told them what had happened—that the house might be saved—but I didn't tell them everything. I wanted to see their faces when I described Mr. Calvert and what he said and everything.

When I hung up, I turned and saw that Grandpa was watching me. He had taken his pipe out of his mouth, and I could tell he was about to say something.

"What?" I asked.

For a moment, he didn't answer.

"What?" I said again. I began to feel worried. Because I could tell that something was coming.

"Jeremy," he said quietly. "You've done a fine job. More than fine. You did what nobody else has been able to do." He took a deep breath. "But there's still more. . . ."

"More?"

He smiled. "Jeremy," he said quietly. "The baby? She'll be here tomorrow."

"What?"

He nodded.

"Mom and Dad, too?" I said. And thought that was the stupidest question I'd ever asked.

"Mom and Dad, too," he said.

"A . . . baby." It was all I could say. I wanted to

see them. Mom and Dad. But not . . . her. Stupid baby Nichole.

"She might be a nice little baby," he said quietly.

I just looked at him. "Yeah," I said, real sarcastically. "*You'll* probably like her."

He laughed. "I don't know," he said. "I haven't met her yet. But I'm willing to give her a chance."

"Good for you," I said.

He only smiled.

19

The rest of that day and the next went by in a blur. The twins were so excited that they couldn't stop talking about the house and how we saved it.

"We did it. We did it," Mimi kept saying. But even though I was happy, I couldn't think about it much. All I could think about was Mom and Dad. And S.B.

I waited until 3:00 the next day, just before I left the twins, to tell them that Mom and Dad might be at Grandpa's.

"Can we come see? Can we come?" they both said at once.

"Yes," I said. "But later."

And then I left them at the corner and took off running toward home. Because I couldn't wait to see them. No matter what, I couldn't wait to see them. Mom. Dad. Were they there yet?

I yanked open the door to the kitchen. They were there—Mom and Dad leaning against the counter, Dad's arm around Mom's shoulders, both of them talking to Grandma, who was doing something at the stove. Everybody turned to me as I came in. I didn't see any baby.

"Mom!" I said. I ran to her and threw my arms around her.

She hugged me tightly, then held me away, looked at me, and hugged me again. "I've missed you so!" she said.

"I missed you, too," I said. I pulled away and looked at her. She looked so good! Mom's real pretty, and I always forget what her face is like when she's gone. I mean, I *know* what she looks like. But I just can't get the picture of her whole face in my mind sometimes.

Then Dad put out his arms, and I turned to him and hugged him, too. He smelled so good—like aftershave lotion and soap. I love my dad. I love them both!

"You surprised me," I said, looking at both of them.

"You surprised *us*," Grandma said before they could answer. "We've just been talking about you. We've been talking about you all afternoon. How did you know about this house? How did you know what to look for?"

I didn't answer. I suddenly felt shy.

I looked at Mom and Dad again. They were home! They were home! And then I looked around for her.

Baby. There was no baby! I turned to Mom. "Where is she?" I said.

"She's here," Mom said, smiling.

I turned and looked where she and Dad were looking—toward the kitchen table.

There, in the middle of Grandma's kitchen table, was this little white carrying thing, sort of like a chair. There was a pillow on either side of it, I guess to keep it from falling off. And in the middle of it was the Stupid Baby.

I looked at Mom and Dad and Grandma, and they just all just smiled at me. But none of them moved toward the table. Grandpa had come upstairs, too, but he was over by the counter, and he seemed to be busy lighting up a pipe again.

I took a deep breath, then walked over to the table and looked at her.

Mom had been right—she *was* little. But she wasn't skinny. She was sleeping, and her little stomach was round, and puffing in and out with each breath. She had a mass of fluffy black hair that stood out all around her little face like she had just stuck her finger in an electric socket. And talk about fingers! How could fingers be that little? She kept opening and closing them in her sleep as though she was having a dream. She was moving her mouth, too, like she was sucking. She must have been dreaming about her bottle.

As if she knew I was standing there watching her, she opened her eyes, her wide, black eyes. I know people say other people have black eyes when really their eyes are just dark brown. But this kid's eyes were black. And then she smiled. She looked right at me and smiled.

I turned to Mom. "She smiled at me!" I said.

Mom came over to the table, and she smiled, too. I turned back to the baby.

"Umm, gug," the baby said. She smiled again and said it again, only like a question this time. "Umm, gug?"

Mom and I both laughed.

And then, as if we had hurt her feelings by laughing at her, she began to cry. She stuck her bottom lip out and screwed up her face, and she began to whimper.

"Oh, don't!" I said. I turned to Mom. "She's going to cry!"

I was right. Just like that, she started to scream. And scream and scream. It was hard to believe that a person that little could make that much noise. Her tiny face was all screwed up, and real tears came out of her eyes.

"Mom?" I said. "Do something!"

But Mom didn't seem too upset about it. Over the baby's screaming, she said, "Would you like to hold her?"

"Me?"

"Yes. It's not hard." Mom bent over and showed me. She slid one of my hands under the baby's back and bottom. It was warm and soft under there. "Now," Mom said. "Just keep your other hand under her neck and head and lift her. That's all."

I did, lifting her out of her carry thing the way Mom showed me. She didn't weigh anything. I shifted her around so she was lying in my arms. And the minute I did she stopped yelling. She was still whimpering a little, though.

"I don't blame you, baby," I said softly to her. "People shouldn't laugh at you when you didn't say anything funny. Right?"

With one hand, I touched her hair. It felt like bird feathers.

Baby Nichole smiled at me again, and tears were still in her eyes. It was like seeing the sun come out during the rain. She sighed and said, "Umm, gug" again.

"You don't have much of a vocabulary," I said.

The timer went off on the stove, and Grandma and Dad started doing something. Mom started to go help them, but then she stopped and said, "Want me to take her from you?"

"Yes," I said. I held her out to Mom, glad to get rid of her. She didn't feel soft and warm anymore. She'd begun leaking.

Mom took Nichole, but first she grabbed a diaper and stuck it between her arm and Nichole's bottom. Yuck.

And then Mimi was pounding on the door. You always know it's Mimi by the way she knocks, like she's trying to beat the door down.

"I'll get it!" I said.

I opened the door, and it was Mimi and Libby.

They came in and looked around the kitchen. The

minute they saw everybody there, they both looked at me, and both of them said the same thing at the same time. "Are you leaving?"

I hadn't even thought of it. I looked at Mom. "Am I?" I said. "Do I have to leave right away?"

"Not yet," Mom said. "Not for a while."

Mimi looked at Mom. She poked Libby. "The baby!" she said.

She and Libby went over to Mom. I went, too. I wondered how Mom could hold Nichole, still all sloppy like that.

"That's Nichole," I said to the twins. And then I said, "Nichole, this is Mimi. And that's Libby."

Nicole stared at them but she didn't smile. She just made a fist of all her tiny fingers and stuffed the fist in her mouth. She began making those sucking movements again, like she was hungry.

"She's cute," Libby said.

"I hope her hair looks better when she gets older," Mimi said.

I just laughed. I didn't think it was so bad.

"Let's go in my room," I said. "We gotta talk." Because I thought this would be a good time to tell them about them maybe coming to my house for the summer.

Mimi and Libby went in my room. But at the kitchen door, I stopped. I turned around and saw that Grandpa was still standing by the counter, right where he'd been before. It seemed like he was waiting for something.

I knew what he was waiting for—me.

I went over to him. "She's okay," I said quietly. "She's soft."

He nodded.

"She is," I said. "And she's got funny hair."

Grandpa smiled.

"Well," I said. "I don't want her. But maybe someday I'll feel different. I might . . . like her."

He smiled again. But he still seemed to be waiting for something.

"You know what?" I said.

"What?" he said.

"I think it's okay. This is where I belong," I said.

Grandpa looked troubled. "You mean—this house?"

"No," I said. "Well, yes, that, too. But I meant something else." Because looking around me, I suddenly realized something. I thought I knew what Grandpa had been talking about that night—when he said that a place where you belong isn't always something you can see. This was my place. With my family. With everybody. I was glad it was here in this house. But I knew now it could be anywhere.

"It's this," I said. I waved my hand around to show Grandpa what I meant—not the room, but the people. Dad talking to Grandma, both of them laughing while they did something at the stove. Mom holding Nichole, who had started to scream again. The twins, waiting for me at the door to my room. And Grandpa, especially Grandpa, standing so close to me, listening to me so carefully.

Grandpa nodded slowly and began smiling at me. And I knew now that he knew I understood.

He leaned in closer to me to hear, since Nichole was screaming again. Only there wasn't anything else I needed to say. But his face was so close to mine that I couldn't resist it—I kissed him real quick on the cheek.

And then I got out of there, away from Nichole's screaming, and into my room to be with my friends.